# DEATH WATCH

SOUL READER SERIES BOOK TWO

## ANNIE ANDERSON

DEATH WATCH

*Soul Reader Book 2*

*International Bestselling Author*
Annie Anderson

Edited by Angela Sanders
Cover Design by Tattered Quill Designs

www.annieande.com

*For the family I wasn't born into but made. I love you to the moon and back.*

BOOKS BY ANNIE ANDERSON

THE ARCANE SOULS WORLD

### GRAVE TALKER SERIES

*Dead to Me*

*Dead & Gone*

*Dead Calm*

### SOUL READER SERIES

*Night Watch*

*Death Watch*

*Grave Watch*

THE ETHEREAL WORLD

### ROGUE ETHEREAL SERIES

*Woman of Blood & Bone*

*Daughter of Souls & Silence*

*Lady of Madness & Moonlight*

*Sister of Embers & Echoes*

*Priestess of Storms & Stone*

*Queen of Fate & Fire*

### PHOENIX RISING SERIES

*(Formerly the Ashes to Ashes Series)*

*Flame Kissed*

*Death Kissed*

*Fate Kissed*

*Shade Kissed*

*Sight Kissed*

## ROMANTIC SUSPENSE NOVELS

### SHELTER ME SERIES

*Seeking Sanctuary*

*Reaching Refuge*

"Alone. Yes, that's the key word, the most awful word in the English tongue. Murder doesn't hold a candle to it and hell is only a poor synonym."

— STEPHEN KING

There were three acceptable reactions to finding a creepy note in your bed from the man who killed your parents.

One: scream your head off and hope someone runs to come save you—*not my favorite option by far.*

Two: smash shit. *On-brand, and really, who can blame me?*

Or three: turn into the ice-cold she-beast that devoured the souls of hundreds of damned arcaners. *I like this one. It has panache.*

I had a solid leaning toward door number two—with the option for three—once I got my shit together. And by shit being together, I meant I needed pants on to deal with this. And maybe a strong cup of coffee and a bag of blood to slake those pesky cravings.

Digging through the ridiculous closet Dahlia had set up for me, I found pajama pants and a top and tossed them on. After that, I began to lose steam as the loss started to creep in.

*Man, I knew I should have just started smashing shit.*

Anger kept my head above water.

Anger kept me alive.

Anger had hauled my ass through a whole year of being a homeless, soul-sucking monster.

Anger was my friend.

Swallowing hard, I reached for the note. The elegant scrawl blurred a little bit as the emotions started hitting in a one-two punch of bullshit I in no way had the mental capacity to deal with.

What had Mom always told me? *One foot in front of the other, Sloane. Keep moving.*

I couldn't remember my parents' deaths. I couldn't remember how I survived the fire that took them from me, or why I'd woken up days later at the foot of my own grave. All I knew was that they were gone, and somehow, I'd remained. Of course, I'd always had an inkling that something had been amiss. I mean, how the fuck else had I ended up in a granny nightgown taking a snooze on my own grave? It wasn't like I put myself there. But until I read that letter, I didn't *know*.

And the knowledge was a hot poker of loss and grief and rage in my gut.

Add in the fact that the man who'd killed them left me a note inside the first home I'd had in a year. In my bed. In this house, a place where I was supposed to be safe.

The burn in my gut only scorched brighter.

A part of me wanted to do the smart thing, which meant taking this note and giving it to Emrys. She'd know what to do, right? Someone who'd been around since time was a baby likely knew more than I did.

Too bad the other part of me screamed to sniff that letter, to take the scent from it and hunt down the man who'd written his lazy scrawl on the cardstock.

But I knew.

I knew if I opened that door, if I pulled that pin, I would lose the tenuous hold I had on my soul. I would lose everything, and I didn't have that much left to lose.

So instead of taking the scent for my own, instead of letting vengeance take root in my belly, and instead of doing the smart thing, I stalked out of my room and down the hall, following Thomas' scent pattern to a nook of the corridor I hadn't been down before.

I couldn't say for sure why I picked Thomas instead of Emrys or Bastian. No, that wasn't right. I could totally say why I picked Thomas over my potential romantic *whatever* and a woman that essentially amounted to my boss.

Thomas knew rage.

He knew vengeance.

And he owed me one.

I didn't even get a chance to knock before Thomas had the door open, his eyes flashing red for a moment before fading back to green. Clad in nothing but a pair of black silk pajama pants, I should have swooned or started drooling or something, but all I could do was hand him the note. And if my hand just so happened to be trembling a little, well, then, that was allowed.

Thomas took the note but didn't look at it. No, he stared at my face. I had no idea what he saw there, but I didn't think it was good.

"You smell of Death himself. Why are you handing me a note written in blood, Sloane?"

His whispered words sounded like a bomb going off. Rage ignited in my chest, and it was all I could do to not shriek in his face.

"Read it," I growled through my teeth, knowing full well that if I opened my mouth, I would start screaming and never stop.

With a fair amount of reluctance in his expression, Thomas' gaze dropped to the card in his hand. It took him less than a second to read the note, and even less than that to vamp all the way out. His sclera went from white to blood-red in an instant, his needle-like fangs peeking out from under his lips. He dropped the card as if it burned him, latching onto my shoulders as if I was a bomb that he was trying to keep from exploding.

At his instant rage, mine ignited as if he'd given me permission to lose it. But whatever he saw next made him move.

In less time than I thought possible, I was up and over Thomas' shoulder, and we were in Emrys' office. I barely got a glimpse of the room before I was bumped off his shoulder and dumped on the leather wingback I'd destroyed with my nails just a few days ago. Then, Thomas, in his ancient wisdom, decided to sit on me.

Cool skin smushed my cheek as Thomas effectively locked me down.

"Thomas, I don't often say this to you, but what the fuck?" Emrys muttered, her tone a mix of baffled and exasperated.

"We have a problem," he replied, the sound of his voice radiating through my whole head from his chest.

"I gathered," Emrys said drolly, the exhaustion in her tone plain as day, even with an ancient vampire using me as a recliner. "Care to share before I have Axel dose you with a tranquilizer?"

"Yes, I fully plan on that, but I'm going to need you to brace yourself, and then I'll get up."

"Bloody fucking hell, Thomas, out with it. I haven't slept in two da—"

Thomas peeled himself from the chair, revealing Emrys in all her tired glory. "Jesus, Mary, and Joseph," Emrys whispered, her odd red irises glowing brightly as she slowly stood from her seat, bracing herself. "Sloane, darling, what's wrong?"

How could I answer her? I'd known something had happened to my parents, but until I'd read that note, I hadn't known it was on purpose. I'd always suspected, sure, but the truth was poison running in my veins, spoiling everything it touched.

"It's this, I think," Thomas replied, handing her the note I'd thought he'd dropped.

The one written in blood.

Whose blood, I had no idea, but everything in me told me I wouldn't enjoy the answer. Everything in me said that the blood on that note would bring me pain and anguish and leave me adrift.

Leave me with nothing.

Emrys didn't break our gaze, even as she took the card from his hand.

"Do you know what you look like right now?" she asked, her expression locked down tight.

Typically unreadable, the druidess held an innumerable number of secrets under that mask, and none of it was comforting. All I could do was grit my teeth as I shook my head. Why in the blue bloody fuck did it matter what I looked like? Why did it matter when she had proof in her hands that my parents were indeed murdered? When she could look at that note and see everything I couldn't bring myself to say?

Nodding to herself, Emrys skirted her giant mahogany desk and held out her hand. When I didn't take it, she latched her fingers on my wrist and gently drew me up from my chair. Leading me to an odd bookcase, she pulled on the spine of a book, and the whole thing moved, pushing back and turning in to reveal an opulent—if a little sparse—room. All that was inside was a bed, a lamp on a lone nightstand, and a full-length mirror.

Emrys tugged me directly to the mirror, turning me to face it, her fingers digging into the skin of my shoulders as if she were trying to hold me in place.

But as soon as I caught sight of my reflection, I understood why Thomas had said I smelled like the dead.

The impossibly white hair and purple eyes were the standard. The fact that my fangs were showing and said purple eyes were glowing like lanterns, also standard—especially since I was a teensy step from losing it.

What was *not* standard was the... I didn't even know how to describe it.

My skin and eyes were radiant, shining with this odd white light that seemed to come from within. But more than that, every few seconds, the figure in the mirror would waver just a little, like a ripple on a pond, and in its place, was what I could only describe as death.

One second my face appeared exactly as I knew it to be. The next, it was as if a skeleton had been superimposed over my features. The creamy-white of the bones winked out every few moments as if it had never been there at all, only to return like a nightmare.

Staring at myself for a solid minute, I tried to get my brain to process what I saw. I was pretty sure my brain broke, remade itself, and broke again in that minute.

I wasn't stupid—contrary to popular belief. It wasn't exactly a leap to suggest that I'd somehow been spelled or hexed or cursed, or whatever the fuck the magic-wielding populace called it. This X, this person who'd taken the time to let me know of his presence, had done this to me somehow. I was sure of it.

He'd killed my parents.

He'd smelled their flesh burn.

He'd...

"Can you fix it?" I croaked, still staring at the mirror and not meeting Emrys' gaze. Both she and Thomas appeared as if they'd seen a ghost. I didn't need another glance at them to see it again.

"I can try, lass."

Emrys left me then, and a few moments later, she bellowed out a curse which had me racing back to the office. She stared at the note as if it had bitten her. Then her gaze slowly drifted back to me.

"That slip of paper should have killed you," she whispered, her face paler than my *Skelator* one. "It is dark magic, forbidden magic. A blood curse." She said it with a frightened sort of reverence that I didn't think would ever come from her mouth. Emrys was resolute. Steadfast. Indomitable. The fear in her voice made bile crawl up my throat.

"Maybe it doesn't work on people like me?" I offered, the feeble suggestion posed as a question. I didn't know the first thing about people such as myself, and the only person I could think to ask wasn't someone I wanted anywhere near me.

"None of this makes any sense. This"—She pointed at the cardstock—"is foul magic. Made from a member of your line. Spells like this were outlawed in the dark ages. With a working like what I see here, a person could wipe out an entire family with just one spell if they had a mind. I can't think of a single reason in the world you should still be standing here breathing." She swallowed audibly, her face draining of all remaining color. Gently, she sat herself down in her leather chair, a trembling hand covering her mouth.

But there wasn't anyone left in my family—no one that I knew. Mom had told me ages ago that she was an orphan, that she'd lost her siblings early on. Then again, Mom had also implied I was human. That she was, too.

Did this mean that this X had to be someone in my family? If what Emrys was saying were true, then he had to be. *Well, fuck.* That thought had a cold pit of dread opening wide in my belly.

"Can you fix it?" Thomas asked, echoing my earlier question and breaking me out of my thoughts.

By the expression on Emrys' face, I didn't think she could. That single expression told me volumes. She had no idea what was wrong with me, she had no idea why I looked like I did, and she didn't have one single clue as to how to fix it.

She steeled herself then, seeming to shove all her emotions down as she erected a wall of assumed calm.

"I can try," she said again, this time with a resolute power that she hadn't possessed earlier.

But I didn't believe her.

Not at all.

## 2

So, there I was, sitting in the middle of a pentagram with Emrys chanting around me as I watched Thomas sip whiskey from a cut crystal tumbler. I grumbled as I held the still-bloody heart of a bull in one hand—*locally bred and humanely sourced according to Emrys*—and an ax in the other. All the while, she was in the middle of the thirtieth such spell to reverse whatever this X had done to me.

"Hush, or she'll have to start over," Thomas chided, sipping his drink as if this weren't the last thing Emrys said she could try before she would have to do some really bizarre shit. This was weird enough, dammit, and I was getting worried there would be nothing for me, other than looking like a fucking nightmare until the end of time. Or until I died—whichever came first.

I wanted to toss this bloody bull heart at his face and go eat. Maybe the ax, too, if I was being honest. I doubted I would actually manage to hit him with either —he moved too damn fast—but it would make me feel better. Starving for both solid food and blood, I was pretty close to losing patience. Luckily, Emrys' words were reaching their crescendo. Her voice rose in volume as the candles surrounding me at the points of the pentagram flared high for a moment before blowing out altogether.

*Shit.*

I'd learned after the fourth spell she'd tried that this was not a good sign. A quick trip to the mirror proved my assumption correct. One second I was Sloane, weird purple eyes and all, and the next...

Growling, I marched right over to Thomas and snatched his whiskey straight out of his hand, downing it in a single swallow. Wordlessly, I held out the glass for a refill. Maybe it was the bloody fingers that no longer held a bull heart or the ax in my other hand, but Thomas quickly filled the tumbler.

After the hours we'd spent researching and trying one spell after the other—each with varying results—her new first order of business would be creating a glamour for me. Mostly so I didn't scare the absolute shit out of people in the house.

"I need a glamour," I muttered, sipping the amber liquid as if it would hold my salvation.

*Do soul-stealing monsters get salvation? Doubtful.* But I was going to finish this whiskey just to check.

"Whoa, there," Thomas grouched, stealing the tumbler back. "That's a seventy-five-year-old Scotch, not a tequila shot. If you want to be a heathen, go drink something else."

I stuck my tongue out at him, blowing a raspberry like the fully functional adult I was. "Like you wouldn't bathe in the stuff if you could."

Thomas seemed to think about it for a moment before conceding with a shrug.

"You are correct, though. You do need a glamour." Emrys sighed before snatching the Scotch out of Thomas' hand and taking a sip. "At least until I can figure this out."

That was if she could even glamour me. If thirty spells didn't cut it, I had my doubts about whether another would work on me at all—even if it were just changing my appearance.

Emrys' odd reddish eyes began to shine as a crackle of power raced across my skin. Evidently, I didn't need to be in the middle of a pentagram with an animal heart in my hand for this one. *Thank fuck.*

She started to mutter in a language I didn't know as

the power died, and then she stomped away, making a beeline for her desk. Her mutterings grew louder as she rummaged through her drawers, searching haphazardly for some item that was supposed to help.

So much for being a functioning member of the team. I mean, how in the hell would I be able to go on missions when I looked this way? How useful would I be if I couldn't read souls *or* go outside? They might as well toss me in the dungeon and throw away the key.

"Ah-ha," Emrys crowed, holding a pendant in her fist like she was making a victory air-punch. "Think you can best me, you wily fuck?" she grumbled under her breath. "I know more than one way to skin a cat."

I really hoped she was referring to this X character and not me. Honestly, I was grateful that she was trying so hard. It had been a long time since someone had gone so far out of their way for me.

Emrys pressed the pendant in between her palms as she hissed in another language I didn't understand, different from the other twelve she'd used so far. Light radiated from between her fingers, almost blinding me before winking out. With an expression of utter satisfaction, she held out the pretty silver pendant with its sizeable oval stone.

"Here, try this out. I might not be able to work any spells on you, but dammit, I can spell objects."

She shook the necklace at me, and I reluctantly took it from her. If this didn't work...

Taking a deep breath, I fastened the silver chain around my neck.

"Holy. Shit," Thomas whispered. "You did it."

Not willing to take Thomas' word for it, I raced back to the mirror. The first thing I noticed was the lack of a skeleton face. But then I realized all too quickly that wasn't the only thing she'd altered. I moved closer to the mirror, as if it would change its answer if I got close enough.

"What the..." I trailed off, trying not to sound unhappy. I didn't look like a creature right out of a nightmare anymore, but...

My purple irises were gone. In their place were vamped-out red ones. And my fangs. Unbidden, my fingers went right for them. Before, my fangs were simply elongated versions of my regular teeth. These needle-like things appeared to be just like Thomas' in the mirror—the weird vampire ones. But as I touched them, I quickly figured out that what I saw in the mirror wasn't real. I might be *seeing* a vampire's fangs, but mine were still there underneath the blanket of Emrys' magic.

Taking a deep breath, I calmed myself enough to retract the fangs, my straight non-pointy teeth reappearing as the vamped-out eyes faded to an odd blue color that was so pale it was barely a hop, skip, and a jump from white.

*Well, at least I won't be walking around looking like an Angler fish all the time.*

"I figured if I was changing things, it might be a good idea to keep your other status away from public consumption," Emrys offered, her tone soft as if she was trying to keep me calm.

I was totally calm. Totally. The calmest calm to ever calm.

"Knowing what we do now, it wouldn't be smart for you to go out looking nowhere near what a vampire should."

That brought back a recent memory of the tiny ABI agent who'd commented on my eyes. I couldn't afford to be stupid—not about that. I took a deep breath—mostly so I wouldn't freak out about the creepy vampire teeth—and gave her a nod.

"That's smart," I croaked, trying to get my voice to work. "If I'm to be Thomas' progeny, it *would* be better if I actually resembled a vampire."

"Exactly." Thomas interjected. "There's no way she'd be able to walk into a nest as she was and pass for one of us."

I hoped I wouldn't be doing that anytime soon. No offense to Thomas, but being in a room full of ancient killers kind of sounded like a bad idea to me. A really, really bad idea. My first kill in this life had been a vampire, and I'd gleaned no illusions about how vampires treated their prey.

"Go get something to eat and a nap," Emrys instructed, breaking me out of my downward spiral of dark thoughts. "We have a mess to clean up tomorrow. And Sloane?"

I yanked my head up from the close inspection of my still-bare feet. "Yes?"

"I suggest you keep this"—She gestured to the room at large—"under your hat for the time being. I'll be looking into how to fix what that blasted note broke, but I need time."

"Of course," I conceded with a nod. I believed Emrys if she said she'd try. But the operative word was *"try."* I highly doubted I'd be going without this glamour any time in the near future.

Maybe ever.

And while she was investigating my dilemma, I'd be looking for X—not that I'd be telling her that. Not that I'd be telling *anyone* that. That little tidbit would also be kept firmly under my hat until I found the bastard. Then it would just be him and me and my fangs.

The real ones.

I kept my face downcast. The last thing I needed was

for Emrys to figure out my plans and stop me. Keeping my shit tight was of the utmost importance until I was safely behind a closed door.

Without another word, I made my exit, leaving Thomas and Emrys behind me as I navigated the hallways to the kitchen, doing my best to stick to the shadows. Though it undoubtedly would have been funny as shit to scare the life out of Bastian—*I mean, he's afraid of a skeleton kitty for fuck's sake*—I wholly intended to avoid the man.

I chose this course of action for two reasons. One—it would be one thing if we knew each other more than a couple of days, but other than a few shared kisses, a house fire, and a battle, I didn't know him from Adam. And he didn't really know me. There was no way I trusted him to let me do what I needed to do. Bastian wasn't precisely a goodie-goodie, but he wasn't on my level, either. There was no way he'd be down for what I'd have to do to get answers.

And two—because it was totally worth repeating: he was afraid of a fucking cat. The next to last thing I needed was Bastian seeing my un-glamoured face and blasting me to kingdom come. It was bad enough I was the Skelly Queen of the Night Watch every few seconds when I wasn't wearing the spelled necklace. I didn't need singed hair and charred skin on top of it.

After scrubbing the blood from my fingers—I managed to snag a couple of chicken drumsticks from the fridge while largely ignoring the plethora of cabinets and giant sink. If I studied the room too hard, I'd fawn all over the architecture and get caught. Naturally, I ate the drumsticks cold because the only thing better than just-out-of-the-grease fried chicken was cold leftover fried chicken. I stood at the opulent kitchen island, sleepily munching my first meal since I couldn't remember when, before tossing the bones in the trash.

My solid food cravings sated, I picked my way back to my room. I really wanted a nap, but I was under no illusion that I would ever be able to sleep in that bed again. I also wanted to sink my fangs into Bastian's neck, wanted his blood filling my mouth as his scent invaded my nose. I wanted to be held and comforted. I wanted to cry my fucking eyes out. I wanted to mourn my parents and how they'd been stolen from me.

But I wouldn't be doing that, either.

Because as soon as I crested the landing, Thomas was fully dressed and waiting for me.

"Get dressed and be ready to go in ten minutes. We've got a job," he informed me, his face a mask of thunder wrapped in an "oh shit" coating.

*Of course we did.*

## 3

I t was all I could do not to throw the mother of all tantrums and stomp my foot. I'd been up since the day before yesterday, lived through a house fire, a ghoul battle, finding out my parents were murdered, and Emrys' bevy of spells. Oh, and discovering I was now the female embodiment of *Skelator*? Yeah, that just added to the tippy top of my "what the fuck" for the week.

Unless someone was about to die a quick and painful death, I wasn't going anywhere. I opened my mouth to say just that, but Thomas cut me off before I could even utter a single syllable.

"Don't. Argue," Thomas growled as he pinched his brow. "I haven't slept either, but you and I are going to Knoxville, and there isn't another way around it. This isn't a message I can deliver via text, and my contact isn't answering her phone."

"What message?"

"I don't know about you, but I don't think the pile of bodies we left in that warehouse is going to go unnoticed for very long. You know, since the cops were descending right about the time we left? Unrest with the ghouls has a way of spilling out through the arcane world. If they think they were slighted or maligned in any way, they typically take it out on their closest rivals, no matter what happened or why. I need to alert my old nest. I owe it to them."

Grumbling, I brushed past Thomas and headed for my room. "You want me to go with you to a nest?" My jaw practically cracked as a yawn hit. "That sounds like the worst idea I've ever heard of. And this is me talking. If I'm the voice of reason in any situation, you should really rethink your priorities."

Thomas gave me a dark chuckle, following me down the hall. "It's a two birds one stone kind of a thing. I have to declare my progeny within the first year. You're already a year old, and if I want to keep the Arcane Bureau of Investigation out of my affairs, I need the queen to sign off on you. With Emrys' glamour, you should be able to pass muster as long as you don't rip anyone's soul from their bodies. Should be a piece of cake."

I was now fully awake, standing stock-still in the middle of the hall as I stared at Thomas. "Are you out of your fucking mind?"

Did I mean to yell that loud enough to wake the dead? No.

Is that precisely what I did? Absolutely.

"What?" he said with a shrug. "It's not as if they're going to make you dine on the blood of the innocent. They won't even look at you too hard. As long as you aren't a feral monster, you should be fine."

This sounded like the worst idea ever concocted in the history of the universe. Huffing, I marched double-time to my room, only to spy Bastian sitting on my bed when I got there.

*So much for avoiding the guy.*

He startled when Thomas and I busted through the door, our commotion knocking him out of what appeared to be a solid snooze.

"How long have you been here?" I asked, praying my voice wasn't as accusatory as it sounded in my head.

Bastian yawned as he stood, an imprint of his fist more telling than anything he'd say. He'd been here for several hours, if not all damn day.

"I don't know," he muttered sleepily. "What time is it?"

I had no idea. My internal clock told me night had fallen already, but other than that, I was at a loss.

"It's eleven," Thomas supplied, impatience laced in his tone. "We don't have a lot of time, Sloane. Toss on one of the ridiculous dresses Dahlia got for you, and let's go."

*Say what now?*

"Dress? You didn't say anything about a damn dress, Thomas."

I'd only just noticed that Thomas was in a black suit with a black shirt and no tie. And back to pinching his brow like I was trying his patience. "I'm taking you to the fucking vampire queen of Knoxville, Sloane," he hissed, his eyes bleeding red but his fangs remaining hidden. "I need you to make a good impression."

I didn't see how stuffing my tomboy ass in a frou-frou dress was going to impress anybody. Thomas seemed to be about a millisecond away from snapping, so rather than arguing, I stomped over to the closet. I hadn't perused the offerings too much in my stay here, the utter lack of time conscious a valid excuse. I hadn't been too interested in fashion prior to my world falling apart. Sure, I appreciated the artistry of it, but jeans and a T-shirt were fine with me.

Blindly yanking a black dress from a hanger, I threw it on, managing to zip it by myself. It was a legit ball gown, one of those lace and chiffon numbers that made everyone resemble a fairy princess. It seemed too delicate a garment for someone like me to wear, with a lace bodice and lined chiffon skirt. Long lace sleeves fit snug to my arms, tied with a black ribbon at my wrists. The deep "V" of the neckline went all the way to my sternum, the nude mesh holding the sides together by a wing and a prayer. And the skirt was something out of a fairytale.

There was no way I wasn't going to mess this up.

I forewent the matching black heels in favor of my lace-up combat boots. *No one will be seeing my feet anyway, right?*

Still grumbling, I stomped out of the closet and hoped Dahlia had supplied me with some makeup, or else I would look like a weirdo. This wasn't the dress for a bare face—even I knew that.

I nearly tripped over my skirt but managed to make my way into the bathroom without injury. Pawing through the drawers, I found a small makeup bag with what I needed. While I was a novice at fashion, I was a master at makeup. It was basically just painting, only on my face. In less than ten minutes, I was done, my eyes screaming drama while my lips were stained the color of blood. There wasn't much I could do with my hair, so this was the best I could do with no notice.

Emerging from the bathroom, Thomas and Bastian's conversation grounded to a halt. Thomas' jaw dropped, but Bastian got an odd, soft look on his face.

"If you tell me I can't take weapons with me, I'm not going," I muttered, planting my fists on my hips. There was absolutely no way I'd be walking into a vampire nest —and in no way actually being a vampire—without weapons. This skirt was enormous. I could fit a Sherman tank under here.

That unfroze Thomas.

"As long as you don't draw them unless you absolutely have to, and you can keep them hidden," he said, nodding to my skirt, his thought following mine.

"Your eyes are a different color," Bastian blurted, and already I felt terrible. There was no way I was telling him why they weren't purple anymore.

Thomas gestured to my necklace. "Emrys made her a glamour so she could pass as one of my kind at presentation. No sense in walking into a nest unprotected."

Bastian nodded, yawning again. "Good call. That would be bad."

"You're staying here and sweeping the house. We need to make sure Booth didn't leave us any surprises.

Harper did a cursory inspection, but you and Dahlia will be reinforcing the warding while we're gone," Thomas said, his tone not allowing any leeway. This was an order.

The exhaustion cleared a little from Bastian's expression as his jaw clenched, but he inclined his head.

"I'll go find Clem," I muttered, skirting around the tense tableau between the two men. I had no idea what was going on, and I didn't have it in me to care.

I had enough to deal with.

But I didn't make it more than a foot past Bastian before he caught my hand in his. Glancing over my shoulder, he snagged my gaze with his own.

"Are you okay?"

Such a simple question, and yet it was a shot right to the heart.

"I'm fine." What else could I say? *My whole world fell apart again for the twelfth time since you met me. Care to help me put the pieces back together?*

"You're not, but when you want to talk to me, just know that I'm here. You're not alone anymore, you know."

Shakily, I gave him a nod and turned back to the door, praying I didn't end up having to fix my makeup.

. . .

Outfitted with only a Glock and a dagger the size of my forearm, I felt barer than naked as I stared at the darkened church. The giant building seemed to melt into the night, the sleepy city of Knoxville buzzing around this dark bit as if it weren't there.

Nestled in what Thomas called Arcane City, the decommissioned cathedral sat like an aging lady, largely ignored yet knowing all the secrets. He'd explained that Knoxville was divided into two parts: the arcane world and the human one. He'd informed me that most places were, unbeknownst to the humans. Arcaners walked among them in secret, blending in, yet staying apart, and had been since the dawn of time. I thought back to the life I'd led prior to waking up in that cemetery and knew he was telling the truth. I hadn't known a damn thing about this world until I'd slammed face-first into it.

This bit, this tiny pocket of Knoxville, was a place no human would dip a toe in. Not because it was dirty or dangerous, but because humans knew when they were being hunted. A leftover signal in their brains that evolution hadn't quite snuffed out sounded when they were being stalked, letting them know they weren't the top of the food chain. Well, that, and I had no doubt this place was warded out the ass.

Vampires clustered around the wide steps of the cathedral leading up to the expertly carved and substantial doors. Thomas had looped his arm through mine and guided me toward them, and I fought the urge to yank up my skirts and sprint away. Not only was I in formal wear, but I was sorely under-armed and at a disadvantage. I knew enough from my time on the streets of Ascension, but not enough about etiquette, social norms, or polite discourse to avoid making a fool of myself.

How to draw, how to paint, and how to fight—those were in my wheelhouse. Dislodging a ghoul's head in less than five seconds? Absolutely. Not offending an ancient arcaner that could eat me for lunch? That part was iffy.

The vampires appeared to still for a moment as they caught sight of us before seeming to stand at attention. As we ascended the steps, each guard we passed knelt, their heads bowed as if a king was walking by. Mouth agape, I stared first at them and then at Thomas.

Out of the corner of my mouth, I whispered, "What the fuck is going on?"

"I'll tell you later," he murmured back, his voice barely audible. "Close your mouth, Sloane. You're catching flies."

*Catching flies, my ass.*

Emrys had implied—*or at least I thought she'd implied*—that Thomas had been kicked out of every nest he'd ever lived in. If he'd been kicked out of this nest, why were they bowing?

I snapped my mouth shut, blanking my expression as if this was no big deal. The goal tonight was not to react. Not to Thomas' apparent status, not to the breathtakingly beautiful cathedral, not to anything. I could totally do this.

A pair of guards opened the giant doors, bowing at Thomas as he guided me through. It was an actual struggle not to freeze at the entrance and stare. But man, did I want to. This place—while definitely what I would consider on-brand for a vamp nest—was one of the most magnificent buildings I'd ever been in. I wasn't particularly interested in other churches, but this cathedral was just a beauty. A gallery of pews sat to the left and right of a wide aisle that led to a raised dais. Vampires filled the seats, dressed similarly to Thomas and me, their voices a low buzz of conversation. More people were sitting in the upper gallery, their opulent gowns and sharp tuxedos a happy reminder that Thomas had my back. Had I walked in here with leather pants and a whip on my hip, I had a feeling I would have been just a touch out of place.

Thomas continued his leading, guiding me down the aisle toward a stunningly severe woman sitting on what appeared to be a throne. Skin paler than death, eyes vamped out in a way that seemed permanent, and painted lips the color of blood, she was the most beautiful and yet most frightening woman I'd ever seen. Dark hair was piled on her head in purposefully haphazard curls, a few tendrils snaking out of the complicated up-do to artfully caress her neck. She wore a brilliant green gown that was so simple, and yet so achingly complex, it had to have cost a fortune.

We reached the end of the aisle, and Thomas bowed his head slightly. I copied him, wishing I would have received an etiquette lesson on the hour-long drive here. All I'd gotten was Thomas' clenched jaw and silence.

"You have some nerve," a woman growled, drawing my gaze from what had to be the queen of this nest to her right.

I quickly realized that the voice did not belong to a woman at all but a child. Pale-blonde hair and blue eyes were set in an elfin face of a vampire who had likely been no more than ten when she was turned. And that had to have been centuries ago. This little whisp of a "girl"—*and I use that word lightly*—had the look of a being older than dirt. Dressed in a black lace confection appropriate for a child beauty queen, she stood from her chair.

She then launched herself at Thomas.

I couldn't exactly say *why* I did it. I mean, she had me

by centuries, and Thomas could take care of himself. But as soon as her feet left the dais, I had the knife Clem had given me yanked from its sheath and was in front of the man in an instant.

Thomas owed me, not the other way around, but he'd been kind to me when I'd needed it, and I wouldn't let him get attacked. No way, no how.

It was as if everyone froze. Conversations halted, guards stood stock-still, and even this slip of a thing stood arrested at the end of my blade, which was poised at her throat.

To this tiny—but by no means less deadly—vampire at the point of my knife, I said, "Settle down there, Blondie, or we're going to have a problem."

I had a feeling we probably already had one.

## 4

**B**londie's expression—which had been full of surprise—quickly stretched into a wide grin. She slid her gaze from my blade to the man behind me. "Oh, I like her. I approve, Thomas. I refuse to let you throw this one back. Did you see how fast she moved?"

Confused but no less wary, I withdrew my blade from her neck and took a step back. Yes, the action gave the illusion that I was standing down, but it still kept me between her and Thomas. Yes, he could defend himself, but something about this place made me think he was more vulnerable here. More at risk. There had to be a good reason he left, right?

"I did. You getting slow in your old age, Ingrid?" Thomas shot back, skirting around me to sweep the small vamp in his arms and give her a hug. Their embrace reminded me of my father's hugs, warm and full of love, and my heart ached a little bit.

"Absolutely not. I'm as fabulous as I've ever been, you fuck."

The curse falling from her childlike mouth startled me for a second before I started snickering. The relief of not having to cut my way out of this nest swept over me. It had been a test—one I hoped I passed.

"You chose well, Thomas. This one will do a magnificent job as your enforcer," the queen said, her smooth voice washing over me.

It was laced in a kind of power I hadn't experienced in my time as an arcaner. It wasn't as if it worked on me exactly, but it flirted with the edges of my brain, seeking entrance. I didn't appreciate being tested like that and couldn't help shooting her a look of contempt, which earned me a no-shit giggle from the queen.

"Yes, you must keep this one. So sound of mind, so strong."

My frown deepened. I didn't enjoy being discussed like I was a slab of beef. But I didn't say anything. We were doing okay for now, and I didn't need to ruin that with my mouth.

"It has been so long since you made a progeny, I thought your days as a sire were over. Tell me—why did you choose this one?" The queen's words were less conversation and more like an accusation. Unbidden of my brain, my hand tightened on the hilt of my dagger.

Thomas stepped away from Ingrid, approaching the queen. "As an uninherit of the Sawyer blood mage line, I felt that Sloane would be a good fit for someone like me. We both are on the outskirts of the arcane world, both without family. It seemed like a no-brainer."

But the queen wasn't looking at him. No, she was looking at me. "And did you turn her before or after her parents were killed in their home and their house burned to the ground?"

*Did she just say that to me? Did she just accuse me of murdering my parents?*

It was all I could do to re-sheathe my blade, but I did it. Because when I knocked her ancient ass out, I wanted it to be with my bare fucking hands.

"I will kindly ask you to shut your fucking mouth about my parents." I seethed through gritted teeth. "Your *Majesty*," I added, sneering.

If I hadn't been wearing the necklace that held my glamour, I'd undoubtedly have bright-purple eyes and fangs at the ready. With the glamour, I had no idea what I looked like. Was I vamped out and murder-y? Was I calm, cool, and collected? Who the fuck knew?

All I knew was, if she said one more thing about my

parents, I was going to start a fight, and I really didn't give a damn if I was in the middle of a nest of vampires or not.

The queen's smile was unexpected, but I really didn't give a shit. Ingrid, I didn't mind, but this woman had officially gotten on my bad side. "Yes, Thomas. Keep this one. She is magnificent. Such control. Barely a year old and already out of her bloodlust phase. Quite remarkable."

"Yeah, yeah. I'm a goddamn miracle. Could you quit talking about me like I'm a slab of beef sometime in the next thirty seconds? I'm getting annoyed."

"There it is," Ingrid crowed. "Bless Lucifer's bouncing balls; I thought she was going to be a stuffy twat. I knew you wouldn't let me down." She slapped Thomas' shoulder and took her seat next to her queen.

Thomas rolled his eyes at the little vamp as the conversation began buzzing again. He held out his arm for me to approach. "Magdalena Dubois, please meet my progeny, Sloane Cabot."

Magdalena blinked at my name. "She won't be taking the nest's name?"

My brain failed trying to recall how nests worked. I knew there was usually a king or queen with several progenies. But my knowledge was limited to Rogues with no real idea of the hierarchy, or that information just didn't stick when I'd drank them down.

"I haven't discussed it with her, and it was not put forth in her contract, so I doubt it. I don't intend to make a true nest, anyway. You know how well it turned out the last time. Plus, there is only room for one Gao nest in the world."

Magdalena seemed appeased by Thomas' answer. "It is a pleasure meeting you, Sloane," she said.

I honestly couldn't say the same. Test or not, I wasn't too keen on being accused of my parents' deaths, nor was I a fan of the goading way she poked at me. Rather than lie, I bowed my head. Honestly, it was the best I could do.

Thomas let out a dark chuckle, shaking his head at me. I was so happy I amused the man. Well, if he wanted me to be something other than myself, he damn well should have told me.

"I would love to discuss an issue with you privately, Your Majesty. If you would be so kind?" he requested, holding his hand out for Magdalena to take. "Give me a minute, Sloane."

*Well, shit.*

I did not want to be left alone in the middle of vamp central—especially after the wringer I'd just been put through. Ingrid sauntered off to speak with a nearby vampire sitting in the front pew, while the rest of the nest stared at me as if I was either fresh meat or a bug to be smashed.

After muttering a hasty "excuse me," I walked back down the aisle and out the door, praying the frigid January air would calm me down. It was funny. Before I entered the nest, the air hadn't seemed to touch me at all, but now that I was by myself, it bit into my skin, my lace sleeves doing little against the winter chill.

That's right about the time I noticed I really was alone. The guards that had clustered on the steps before were gone—the buzzing quality of activity now a blanket of silence that sent a shiver of unease racing down my spine. Something told me that they should still be here. Something told me that this silence was wrong.

I barely managed to move in time. The hand that reached for me nearly closed around my hair before I was up with the Glock in my hand. Going for my gun was a stupid move—especially in light of the creatures who'd just decided to play. Seven hulking ghouls were fanned out in a semi-circle, their giant bodies blocking off any escape. There weren't enough bullets in the world to make a dent in these fools. With the cathedral walls at my back, my only options were moving to the dark alley to my left or staying put. And I didn't take a shine to either one.

Not. At. All.

Plus, these guys didn't resemble regular, everyday ghouls, either. Oh, no. They were *made* ones who'd been selected for their size and turned—maybe of their own free will, or perhaps not. Nary a one of these bastards were smaller than six and a half feet tall, and all seven of them were wider than a brick shithouse. There was no way I'd get to the door of the nest—not that I'd choose that avenue, anyway. I'd been a complete fucking fool to grab the Glock.

Guns were loud.

They were messy.

And even though we were in a "hidden" part of Knoxville, I didn't exactly think shooting someone in the face right next to a public street was going to win me any favors.

Still, it was what I had.

The first two bullets went into the center ghoul's eyes, hopefully allowing for enough of a distraction as he fell so I could grab the dagger sheathed under my skirt. In my first stroke of luck of the night, my hand closed around the dagger's hilt before they managed to realize what I'd done. And in my second, I had that blade out and at the ready before they struck. Then it was a whirling dervish of moves and countermoves.

I supposed the fear should have lasted longer, should

have made me freeze or something, but it didn't. After the day—*no, the year*—I'd had, I'd been aching to fight someone, anyone. And after the unmitigated rage caused by Magdalena Dubois?

I'd never been so happy to decapitate someone in my fucking life.

The dagger was a bit too short for this task, but I made it work. My blade slashed and stabbed with abandon as I held off the group, while taking the first head at the point of my teeth. It didn't matter what the rest of the world saw with Emrys' glamour, I still had my fangs, and the bastards were sharp.

The only way to kill a ghoul for real was to take the head or burn their bodies to ash, and I really didn't have the time to sit for a bonfire, not with five still-standing ghouls and no backup. But again, the fear I probably should have been feeling never came. No, I was practically giggling as I tossed the first severed head at the next ghoul, the impact of his friend's dome smacking his enough to knock him ass over tea kettle.

This was fun. I'd forgotten how much fun fighting was when I wasn't worried about who lived and who died. When I didn't care for anyone but myself. When all the reasoning I needed was vengeance and the will to survive.

That thought was probably depressing, but at that moment, I just didn't care.

A flash of blonde hair had my giggle dying for a second, until I realized it was Ingrid coming for the assist. Before I could even say anything, Ingrid mowed through the ghouls like a tiny blonde missile, bowling two over before perching on their chests to neatly remove their heads. It was tough not to pout at her taking two heads before I had time to blink.

They had attacked me. It was my fight, and she was ruining my fun. I didn't care if we were on her turf.

Before I could call foul, she'd taken the remaining two down, fluttering her fingers as ghoul heads landed on the pavement with a squelching thud.

And then she was staring at me as if she'd just seen a ghost.

Why on earth would this tiny little assassin look at me like that unless... I slapped my hand to my chest, feeling for my necklace and coming up empty.

*Shit.*

Well, that secret lasted less than twenty-four hours. The jig was up.

## 5

I ngrid seemed to be seconds away from blowing her top. She opened her mouth, sputtering in utter horror as she took a few steps backward. I couldn't exactly blame her. Even Thomas had lost his poker face when he saw my new look for the first time. I had a feeling that hardly ever happened. Holding up a finger, I searched the ground for my missing necklace, hoping to stave off her freak-out until I was back to a semi-normal appearance.

The silver metal winked from the still fingers of the first ghoul who'd reached for me. In my haste to get away, I must not have felt him yank on the chain. Stomping over to him, I snatched the pendant from his hand, fiddling with one of the bent O-rings before clasping it back around my neck.

"What the fuck was that?" Ingrid breathed, her voice barely above a whisper.

The ghoul at my feet—the one I'd only managed to shoot—began to stir. I held up a finger again. "Hold, please. I'm sure all your questions will be answered, just..."

How in the hell could I explain what I was about to do? Figuring I couldn't in the scant time I had before he woke all the way up, I skipped it in favor of getting all the shocking done at once. Ingrid hadn't seemed the excitable sort, and I was really hoping she didn't start screaming her head off.

Stomping on the ghoul's chest, I effectively pummeled his heart before I went for his neck. I needed answers, and the only way I was going to get them was from his blood. It helped that I really didn't give a damn if I took his soul or not. That I had to put on a dress was bad enough, but making me fight in the damn thing was just beyond the pale.

My fangs cut into his cold flesh like a knife through warm butter. His oddly metallic blood was disgusting, leaving a bitter taste on my tongue. But it was his memories that really made my stomach turn. This ghoul wasn't a prince by any stretch of the imagination. A rapist, a murderer, and that didn't cover what he'd done to his own family. This man was nothing like the ghoul I'd refused to drink down in the warehouse.

*Huh. Had that only been a day ago?*

But this ghoul had seen a flash of purple light and a hooded figure, too, just like the ones who'd been working with Booth. I ripped my fangs from the ghoul's neck, spitting out his disgusting blood on the pavement.

It didn't make any sense.

How had they found me here? And why were they looking for me in the first place? Were they even looking for me? Or was it Thomas they were after?

I knew I wasn't going to get anything out of this guy. The mage or witch or whoever had sent him, knew how to cover his tracks.

And it all led back to X.

Irritated, I clutched the ghoul's head in my hand and roughly snapped his neck. Ripping it from his shoulders took less effort than it took to decapitate a Barbie Doll. No sense in letting him come back for seconds.

"What." Ingrid paused, her voice turning shrill. "The fuck was that?" Wide-eyed was not a look I'd ever peg for the tiny vamp. Childlike or not, Ingrid had seen some shit over the years. I'd bet everything I owned—which wasn't much—that she was roughly the age of dirt.

Shrugging, I let the head drop to the pavement. "I needed answers."

My response did not appease her in the slightest. "And drinking his undead blood was going to give them to you?"

I wiped at my mouth with the back of my hand before shuddering a little. "Not exactly."

All things considered, I probably should have chomped down on that ghoul's soul while I was at it, but I just couldn't bring myself to do it. His blood was like swallowing hot garbage.

"Does Thomas know about this?" she asked, gesturing a hand to encompass me, the rapidly decaying ghoul, and likely all that had transpired in the last few minutes.

I winced as I contemplated just how much to tell her. I figured she and Thomas were close, but if I told her, she could haul off and tell the ABI, and Thomas and I would really be screwed. And it wasn't as if I could kill her. Several centuries old or not, there was no way I'd be able to get past the whole looking like a child thing.

"I do," the man in question affirmed, making both Ingrid and I nearly jump out of our skins. He placed his body in between me and Ingrid, protecting me just as I'd done for him. He glanced at me over his shoulder. "She saw?"

"Oh, yeah," I muttered, nodding. I wanted to say sorry, but this was totally not my fault. Well... I supposed if I hadn't gone off gallivanting by myself, this might not have happened, but it wasn't as if I had a neon sign over my head begging people to attack me. How was I supposed to know?

Thomas' expression was not amused, and I had a feeling I would be paying for this later.

"Are you kidding me?" Ingrid hissed. "Did you really just waltz in here and expect that no one would ever find out?"

Up until I got attacked, she and her queen had been singing my praises. We likely could have skipped on out of here had I not taken that breather.

"Of course I did." Thomas sighed, rubbing the back of his neck, discomfort stamped all over him. "Had Sloane's glamour not come off, no one would be the wiser."

*The first order of business: get the necklace fixed so it can't come off willy-nilly. Second: send Thomas a fruit basket or something for tanking his life.*

"Even me?" Ingrid's voice was small, as if the kept secret hurt her, her childlike voice practically stabbing me in the heart.

*Shit.*

Thomas sighed again, pinching his brow. "It's not my secret to tell, Ing."

Now I really felt terrible. Ingrid was someone

Thomas really cared about. I couldn't just waltz off and give her nothing, not after what she saw. "Tell her, Thomas. She knows most of it already. And the rest isn't too far of a stretch to figure out."

And this was how I ended up sitting in the middle of the nests' graveyard, under a spelled cone of silence, nursing a blood bag like a Capri Sun as Thomas told Ingrid my sordid little tale.

Ingrid paced between the graves as she plaited her hair, the long strands sifting like silk in her fingers before she brushed them out and started again. "You're telling me you just woke up like this one day?"

I shook my head. "Not exactly. I didn't use to have the skeleton face thing going on, but the rest? Pretty much. One day I was a normal girl, going to college and irritating my mother, and the next, I was a blood-drinking soul eater with a proclivity for killing bad guys. There's a bout of homelessness and some trial-by-fire murder in there, but that's about the gist."

She stopped her pacing, crossing her arms over her narrow chest as she appraised me. "And this X guy—wait, is it a guy?"

"No idea," I muttered. I slurped the last drops of blood from the bag before removing my makeshift straw and sucking up the last of the blood from the tube. I stabbed it into my last bag, disappointed that Axel and Thomas had been right about the bagged blood situation. It was in no way as good as the molten heat that flowed in Bastian's veins—not by a long shot.

But swill or not, this blood was about a zillion steps above the ghoul's, and I was starving.

"His note had a solid penis-wielding flare to it, so I'm going with guy."

She gave my assessment a nod and continued, "So, this X guy is the man who murdered your parents."

*Wow, that still hurt hearing out loud.*

"I think so." I thought about it for a moment while sipping my beverage. This bag could use some vodka, if I was being honest. "I don't remember who or what killed them, but if he went to the trouble of announcing himself like that, I'm willing to give him the benefit of the doubt."

"Then how did he know you were here?" she asked.

And that was the sixty-four-million-dollar question. One I didn't have an answer to, but I could venture a guess.

"That's a good question, Ing," Thomas said. "I didn't tell anyone outside of my team where I was going. The only other people who knew were you and Mags. I think you have an internal problem."

Thomas' assessment was as brutal as it was accurate. Though, it wasn't as if the Night Watch hadn't been breached before. We were still smack-dab in the middle of the last one.

"Didn't you just tell me one of your own betrayed you? I know with our history, you're hesitant to trust anyone in this nest, but get real." Ingrid knifed her hand through the air, pointing to me. "Someone could have tracked her. This X guy could have tracked you. It isn't out of the realm of possibilities here. Let's not point fingers before we have some hard evidence."

I was piling a lot of trust onto Ingrid's shoulders, so I tried to give her and her assessment a fair shake. But if Thomas was wary of the vampires here, I figured it was smart to keep my eyes peeled.

"I'm not pointing fingers—or at least I'm not trying to. All I'm saying is that you need to keep your eyes open. Keep some important shit under wraps for the time being, or send out false leads. See if there's a leak. If there isn't, no harm, no foul."

Ingrid recrossed her arms, huffing, resembling the eight-year-old girl she most definitely was not. "Fine. But if nothing pans out, I reserve the right to rub your face in it."

Thomas held up a hand as if he was swearing on a bible. "Duly noted."

Softening a bit, Ingrid walked the few paces to hug Thomas, her small head barely reaching his sternum. "I miss having you around. Tell me again why you moved out?"

"Because I enjoy breathing, remember?" He chuckled, giving her a squeeze.

"Oh, that's right." Ingrid huffed before pulling away to level Thomas with an expression full of pure steel. "You stay breathing, you hear me? And keep a lid on that one. All it takes is one idiot with the wrong information to utterly and completely fuck up your whole life."

Thomas' smile turned rueful, and I couldn't help but mirror him. I'd fucked up tonight. I hadn't made sure I was protected, didn't have the right weapons, and hadn't been paying attention. If I ever planned on going outside by myself ever again, I would need to get my shit together.

That was if Thomas let me out of his sight ever again.

"That's the plan," he replied, turning the skull ring on his right hand in a full circle and breaking the makeshift dome of silence.

The ring had been a gift from Simon and made it so nothing living or dead could spy on the wearer. When it came to cool gadgets, I wanted something like that. If I wanted to stay off this X's radar, I'd need all the help I could get.

"And you," Ingrid barked, which made my gaze snap to her. "Watch his back. Do you hear me?"

All I could do was nod. Crossing Ingrid seemed bad for my health.

## 6

TWO MONTHS LATER

"Haunting rooftops again, I see," Bastian called from behind me, startling me out of my intense stare-down of an inanimate object, namely, a door.

The only thing special about this door was that behind it lay a raging arcane club. The music radiated up from the ground, through the building, rattling my bones even from across the street, but that door was nothing more than a metal barrier to the world beyond. I'd always wondered what went on in clubs like those. Would it be sex and alcohol and dancing bodies—*which wasn't much different from a human club in that scenario*—or would it be darker? Blood and death and all the dark things about the arcane world that I hated? I was smart enough to know that the human world had its darkness, too, but it seemed the more I lived in this world, the more I realized that what I thought was evil didn't even begin to scratch the surface.

"It's a hobby," I muttered, shaking my head to clear the dark thoughts as I stretched from my crouch, my joints protesting loudly. One thing about this life that was the same were the aches and pains. I'd sat in one spot too long, staring at that stupid metal door to that stupid arcane club that wouldn't provide any more answers than the last one had.

My search so far had given me one dead end after the other, and after two straight months of nothing, I was starting to get annoyed. It was bad enough that I had the habit of haunting rooftops *before* the man who'd killed my parents left a note on my pillow.

Now, it was an obsession.

In the last two months—in between bounties and training—I'd been scouring every nook and cranny of Ascension. And my questioning methods hadn't exactly been in line with what I would call pleasant.

Bloody would be a better descriptor.

Hopping off the ledge, I knocked the dark hood from my white hair, letting the spring air cool me down. Sweltering under my lightweight jacket, I yanked it off, trying not to rip the fabric. Clem would be pissed if I ripped another one, and as the house's weapons keeper and person in charge of my solid food intake, pissing her off would not be a smart move on my part. Plus, if Bastian found me, there would be no more sleuthing tonight, and the need to hide my beacon of a hair color was no longer necessary.

I'd need to pick harder to find locations if I wanted him off my ass. Well... I kind of wanted him on my ass, just not while I was in the middle of my special project. I stared down at the skull don't-find-me ring I'd conned Simon into making for me. Leave it to Bastian to find a way to work around Simon's magic.

Bastian stood in the darkness, the faint light barely kissing the high points of his face and leaving the rest in shadow. To everyone else, he was a bruiser with his heavy dark brow and bulking frame. To me, he seemed akin to a big teddy bear—a giant, angry teddy bear, but one, nonetheless.

Even if he was spoiling my stakeout.

"Some hobby," he groused, snagging my hand and reeling me in. "You know, instead of skulking around, you could actually go inside one of those clubs. Take a night off from your 'creature of the dark' persona and actually have fun."

*Fun.* It was a struggle not to audibly scoff and even harder not to show the derision on my face. I hadn't had *fun* in ages. Hell, I didn't even know what that word meant anymore. And I couldn't remember the last time I'd taken a night off—definitely pre-orphanhood, for sure.

"'Creature of the dark?' What am I, a *Batman* villain? Do I get a cool costume? Is there a car in this deal?"

Bastian's smile gave me legit butterflies, the wide, white pull of his full lips making me all giddy.

*Ugh, hormones. Why must you betray me like this?*

"No, but it comes with a fabulous house, and our Alfred knows how to make biscuits from scratch."

Just the thought of Clem's cooking made me ravenous. How long had it been since I'd actually sat down at the table and eaten with my housemates? Far too long would be my guess.

"Fair enough," I conceded with a shrug. "Too bad about that car, though."

Truth be told, I'd stolen a crotch rocket from the Night Watch's garage. Well, "stole" was a harsh term. I fully intended to bring it back with a full tank and zero scratches when I was done with it. I had a feeling it was Thomas', and just the thought of damaging the bike made me want to throw up. It wasn't as if I had much in the way of money in my pocket to repay the man, and he was already sticking his neck out for me.

Bastian pulled me closer before making a one-two-step move and spinning me out as if we were dancing instead of just talking. "How about it? Let's go take a night off. Just you and me."

I couldn't remember the last time I'd been to a club, but it was definitely before I was legal to drink, and it was most certainly less cool than any arcaner club. Not that I'd ever been in one of those either, but if it wasn't death and murder, it would probably be okay, right?

"We haven't been alone together in months, Sloane. With Simon getting off house arrest and all those big jobs, it's been crazy. Just one night. The world will not implode if you take the night off, I promise." Reeling me in, our bodies collided enticingly, the gentle rub of his chest against mine doing the bulk of the convincing.

He was referring to the three Fae bounties we'd gone after last month. They had caused so much trouble, I would rather lock myself in the dungeon than go after another of that kind of arcaner again. *Fucking Faeries.*

Bastian dropped a kiss to the bend of my neck, and I had to suppress a shudder. There hadn't been much time for relaxing in the last couple of months and even less time for any kind of romance. Slowly but surely, he was edging back under my skin, making a home for himself there.

It almost made me feel like shit for not telling him about the note. *Almost.*

Then I remembered the shitstorm that followed

the "note of doom" and thought better of it. The less Bastian knew, the better.

"If we must," I conceded as if I had no desire at all to see the inside of the club. I totally did, but for some dumb reason, I didn't want Bastian to know that. "One night off couldn't hurt."

After some kind of secret handshake with the doorman, Bastian led me inside the loudest freaking building I had ever been in in my life. Strobe lights bounced off the walls as the dance music I'd only felt outside pumped through unseen speakers. A mass of bodies writhed on the dance floor while others lingered at the bar or in the booths, yelling to be heard over the din.

The bar was a battered monstrosity with nicks and dents as if it had seen some shit, while the booths were made up of painted black wood and vinyl. There didn't seem to be cocktail waitresses or fancy drinks—just beer in pitchers and baskets of food. I wasn't mad at the modest fare either. The thought of a beer and a basket of fried yumminess—and maybe a blood chaser—seemed like just the thing.

The scent of clean sweat, beer, food, and magic masked everything else, and on top of the noise and light show, I had a hard time figuring out what kind of arcaners we were dealing with. None of them seemed to pay us any mind as Bastian led us right to the dance floor, weaving through the masses to get to the center. The heavy thrum of the bass notes ricocheted through my chest as the heat and music seemed to race down my limbs.

Once Bastian found the perfect spot, he drew me to him, and I quickly learned that he didn't just know how to dance. He knew how to *dance*. I'd never seen a man as big as Bastian have even a lick of rhythm, but all it took was one roll of his hips to realize I'd been sorely mistaken. The sultry beat hit with the punch of a spell, and I quit giving a shit about pretty much anything else except the heat of Bastian in my space and how our bodies fit together. His giant hand found a home on my hip, his fingers flexing just a little, which reminded me of other times...

Times when I had my fangs in his neck and his body in my space and the heat of his blood rushing into my mouth. It reminded me of how good it felt to taste him. To feel his warmth, his soul, to see all the hungry, dirty things he thought about but would never share.

The scent of his need filled my nose as our bodies swayed to the beat, the brush of his chest against mine making my mouth water. I hadn't taken Bastian's blood since our foray in Axel's lab right before a significant facet of my life blew apart. Since then, it had been bad guys and bagged blood for me, which was akin to going from a melt-in-your-mouth medium ribeye to an elementary school cafeteria pizza.

And he smelled good enough to eat.

Something must have flitted across my expression because Bastian's face seemed to mirror everything I had roiling in my chest. The hand at my hip found its way to my hair, and then his mouth was on mine, our tongues dancing rather than our feet.

*Did I even have feet? Did it matter?*

The heat of the club—of Bastian—wrapped me up in a cocoon. In this tiny spot on the planet, in the circle of Bastian's arms, I was safe. I wasn't wrong or weird or different.

I wasn't a monster.

I wasn't a freak of nature.

And then his mouth broke from mine only to travel to my ear.

"Bite me," he whispered, the words hitting me with the force of a wrecking ball. How I managed to hear them over the music, I had no idea. "Please. I've missed you."

The whole of my belly dipped as everything inside me clenched. I'd dreamt about his blood in my mouth, about our sweaty bodies writhing together as I drank from him. I wanted all of it, all of him, and I couldn't toss up another reason I should keep him at a distance.

All it took was a teensy rise on my tiptoes and a slight turn of my head. Then his neck was right there. Every reason I had, every single good intention, went right out the window. Before I really gave my brain the go-ahead, my fangs were in his neck, pulling deep draws from his vein. It was as if I'd been starving for years and he'd given me my first meal.

His need rose around us like a cloud of ambrosia as images bombarded me: strands of my white hair sifting through his fingers, his mouth everywhere he could reach as we writhed together. I wanted every part of his thoughts. I wanted to do every single dirty, filthy, fucking awesome thing I saw and then some. I wanted us out of this club, out of this city, and on a bed that could take a beating.

But before I could remove my fangs from Bastian's neck to tell him just that, rough hands yanked me away from him.

And the last thing I saw before the shit really hit the fan was a blue ball of magic headed right for me.

*Super.*

## 7

The crackling ball of bullshit hit me square in the chest before I even had time to move, the force blowing me off my feet and into the still-dancing crowd. My landing was unforgiving, people kicked and shoved at me as I tried to get a lock on how to move my limbs. The electricity in that spell was enough to take down a rhino, so getting the signals to work took a second—one I really didn't have.

Groaning, I managed to stand, my limbs none too happy about the demand to move. But I didn't get too much down time since another orb of stupid magic was headed right for me. The whole situation pissed me off to no end. I was in the middle of the best time I'd had in months and this asshole ripped it away from me?

No. *Fuck, no.*

My gaze flitted around the room as I dodged the orb —finding Bastian was my highest priority. A close second was finding the bastard who ruined my fun and making them eat their own teeth. My eyes snagged on Bastian, his hulking frame on the other side of a sizable crowd of arcaners swarming toward the exit. His neck was still bleeding, the shine of it making my heart lurch. I hadn't been able to close his wounds. I couldn't say why, but tears pricked my eyes for a second before a surge of heat washed over me.

Bastian was mine. His blood was mine. His body was mine. His safety was mine. Whoever had ripped me from him was going to wish they had never been born.

The mage in question stepped into the light to make himself known, another glittering orb hissing in his hand. The blue magic cast eerie shadows on his face, likely making him appear far more sinister than it should. The guy looked no older than twenty at a push, but I knew he had to be at least a century if not more. Long, scraggly hair pulled into an unfortunate queue at the back of his head, the guy probably snagged a lot of tail in a place like this. With the whole "flannel and ripped jeans and wannabe James Dean but failing miserably" vibe, dumb youngsters of all kinds probably ate it up.

I had never been one of those youngsters, though—even at twenty-three.

"Your kind isn't welcome here. I don't give a shit what your *queen* says. You come into my bar, and use your bloodsucker voodoo on one of my patrons, and you think you're just going to walk out of here? I don't think so."

I knew for a fact I was going to walk out of this bar. The real question was whether or not he would. But mage-dude didn't wait for me to answer. No, he just lobbed that stupid electricity at me like an asshole. Stepping to the side, the magic sailed past me, but he was ready for that. Three more orbs rocketed toward me with the speed of a missile.

Too bad for him, I'd been training.

Before he could throw another one, his wrists were trapped in one of my hands while the fingers of the other were around his throat.

"Considering I had consent, yeah, I do think I'm walking out of here." I squeezed his wrists together to show him I could crush them if I wanted to. With fear stamped all over his face, my bloodlust and vengeance died a quick death, and I sighed.

*Fine. He can live.*

"Look, man. I have no problem with you protecting

your patrons. But just as a request? Maybe don't shoot first and ask questions later."

And then this fucker did the dumbest thing he could have possibly ever done. Instead of nodding and squashing the situation, he decided to spit in my face.

Fun fact: this wasn't the first time that had been done to me in the last year. It turned out that when certain arcaners found out that they weren't at the top of the food chain, they got a little *testy*. So, I showed them what testy really looked like.

With a quick tightening of my fingers, I crushed the mage's wrists. *Let's see him lob anymore orbs for the next little while.* His whole body went slack—an unfortunate move for him, since I still had a hold of his throat. His eyes popped wide as his lack of oxygen finally registered. And all the while his spit ran down my cheek.

His feet scrabbled for purchase on the floor, but I decided being an asshole was more fun, raising my arm just enough that he could only find the barest of relief.

"Now, what did we learn?" I asked, my voice a deadly calm.

His eyes bugged out of his head as his face purpled. Rolling my eyes, I lowered my arm an inch, letting him get a little oxygen. Not enough, but some.

"Fine, I'll answer for you. You learned not to fuck with people stronger than you. You learned that you shouldn't escalate a situation with stupidity—especially when you're at a disadvantage. Now, do I need to kill you, or are you going to finally be smart?"

His gaze flitted to the right before he smiled. "Fuck. You."

He might as well have waved a huge red flag in my face to signal that his backup had arrived.

"Sticking with stupidity, I see." And I'd thought it was going to be such a quiet night.

The thing was, I didn't want to kill this guy. He was just an idiot that wanted to make sure his patrons weren't getting violated. That, I totally understood. After my brush with the Knoxville vampire queen, I got it. Had I been anything other than what I was, she could have gotten me to do anything she wanted to. From what I'd gleaned from Thomas, that ability wasn't just limited to her. It wasn't a surprise that a lot of arcaners were iffy around vamps, but this was just ridiculous.

Without much deliberation—mostly to prevent his backup from getting the upper hand—I tossed the mage in the direction I thought they would be coming from. Well, "tossed" was a more polite term for what I actually did. What I really did was spin in a quick circle and shot put his dumb ass as hard as I could.

It was only fair. He'd blown me off my feet once already, and had I been something else, he would have killed me with one of those stupid balls of electricity. Had I actually been a vamp, it might have done some real damage.

When Bastian brought me to this bar, I'd thought we'd have a nice time. Now I was desperately trying not to murder people.

But the small contingent I'd thought the mage had for backup didn't quite encompass all the people at his disposal. By the time I turned to find the exit, there was enough magic headed my way to flash fire a deity. I tried to run, but it seemed as if I'd hit an invisible wall, a spell of some kind holding me in place as the threat rocketed toward me. Just when I thought I was toast, the magic seemed to hit the same wall I was stuck behind, exploding against it with enough force to rock the whole building.

And then I wasn't trapped anymore. Instead, I was behind a very broad back as Bastian put himself between the mages and me. I couldn't explain the sheer amount of relief I felt at seeing him upright and breathing—even if that relief was seriously tempered by the scent of his still-bleeding neck.

Multicolored magic swirled up his arms as the building trembled beneath our feet.

"I suggest you stop this foolishness before you really piss me off," he growled, the sheer power rolling off his body enough to show them he meant every word he said.

*I probably shouldn't be as turned on as I am right now, right?* I mean, this was a serious situation that required focus and attention so we didn't die. Why exactly did I want to rip his clothes off again?

"Vampires aren't allowed here, and you know it, Cartwright. I don't give a shit who you are, this is still my club." It was the James Dean wannabe speaking, his raspy voice a testament to the fact that I did not, in fact, crush his windpipe.

*Pity.*

"Tell me—who owns this building, Jarek? Who owns this block? Whose property are you on? You do not own this establishment. I do. And if I want to let my woman feed from my neck, I shall. If I want to grant her entrance onto my property, I shall."

*Ho-ly shit.* No wonder the doorman had just waved him in. Bastian owned this place?

"This is my club," Jarek insisted. "I get a say at who comes in."

Bastian's magic burned hotter, and I took a small step back. "This is not your club. You manage the bar. This is my club, my bar, my property. And not only did you let loose potent magic in the middle of a crowd, you spit in my woman's face."

I was tempted to just let Bastian lose it on this fool. Really, really tempted.

The best I could do was put a gentle hand on his back and pray that did something. As soon as I did, though, Bastian shot a look over his shoulder. *Nope, that totally did not work.*

Jarek wasn't the only one in deep shit. I had the distinct feeling I was, too.

I lifted my hands in surrender, and Bastian turned back to the mages in front of him. "You're fired. If I see you inside this club again, you're dead." Bastian shifted his gaze to the other men that had come to Jarek's aide. "Be very careful who you consider friends in this town, gentlemen. Quite frequently their stench can carry, landing on any that help them."

That was a carefully worded threat and warning all rolled into one. I had a feeling Jarek wouldn't be welcome in a lot of places in the near future.

"You can't do that!" Jarek protested, the crackle of his power announcing itself.

I took that opportunity to step to Bastian's right— still behind him so he wouldn't get fussy—but with a clear shot if I needed to help. Bastian wasn't just facing off a few mages. Oh, no. He was facing off against the lowly Jarek and about twenty of his closest pals.

But only Jarek was holding an orb of magic. The

others appeared as if they were trying to surreptitiously find the exit.

"You don't just get to come in here and kick me out. Not after all these years."

With that, Jarek tossed his orb of magic, his failing wrists making the fact that he could do any spells at all a freaking miracle. Though, this probably would have been more impressive if Bastian hadn't plucked the orb out of the air like he was catching a whiffle ball. The electricity fizzled out as Bastian's fingers closed around it, the faint scent of ozone the only sign that the magic had existed at all.

"I do, and no amount of time in my employ would ever excuse what you did. You just painted a target on your back, Jarek. I'll give you a five-minute head start."

Jarek's face went white as he scrambled back, knocking into his friends as he tried to find the door. His friends bolted for the opposite exit. My guess was they wanted Bastian to follow him and not them. Smart.

And then we were alone, but I was under no illusion the threat had passed.

Bastian turned to face me, his expression thunderous. He drew a handkerchief from his pocket, wiping my cheek.

The relief from that simple gesture was seriously

short-lived when he began to speak. "Did you know that certain elements disrupt spells temporarily?"

It didn't matter if his voice was the softest of velvet, my stomach still dropped to my toes.

Slowly, I shook my head.

"What is under that glamour, Sloane?"

## 8

I in no way wanted to answer that question. In fact, I wanted to find a quiet corner and vomit my guts up before running away and never looking back.

That exact moment was something I'd been dreading for months. Bastian saw me. I knew he had. He'd seen what I looked like now. Oh, no.

Bile rose in my throat as I took a step back. I could totally deny it. *I could.* I could also boss up and tell him and stop fucking hiding.

Both options seemed shitty.

"What did you see?" I croaked, my voice a small, pitiful thing. *Dammit, why was telling him what happened so freaking hard?*

Tears pricked at my eyes, and I couldn't help dropping my gaze to my feet. I wasn't this small, frightened girl. I hadn't been in a long time. So why was I doing this dumb shit now?

Bastian moved into my space, reaching for the necklace that held the spell. And even though I'd had Emrys reinforce the clasp with a fair bit of magic, Bastian still managed to unfasten it from my neck.

And I'd let him.

*Stupid, stupid, stupid.*

I'd thought I wanted to throw up before. Now, I just wanted to run and hide. Letting my hair fall in a curtain wasn't going to work either because his fingers were in the strands, and he was tilting my face up so he could inspect it.

"What happened?" he asked, the gentleness in the question ready to break me in two.

I did my best to memorize the open expression on his face because I knew once I told him—*and I had no choice but to tell him*—he was never going to look at me the same way again.

But when I opened my mouth to do just that, nothing came out. I hadn't been scared of anything in so long, and this wasn't exactly a small thing. This was—*he was*—important.

"Let me tell you what I know," he began, granting me a reprieve. "The morning after you helped me save my brother, you got that glamour. The spell work has

Emrys' signature. You've been avoiding me, my brother, his cat, and everyone else in the house except for Thomas. You work and train until you can barely stand up, and when you aren't doing that, you're out prowling Ascension, searching for something. You refuse to come to me for feedings, to talk, or for anything other than the minimum required interaction so I won't get suspicious."

When he put it like that, I sounded like the biggest bitch on the planet, and he should toss me in the garbage the first chance he got.

"Something happened somewhere in the time we got home to when I woke up in your room, I just don't know what it is. And I won't know, and I can't help unless you tell me."

He was being so kind—so levelheaded—about this that I wanted to crawl under a rock and stay there until I felt less like a slug.

"Wh-when I got home, there was a note on my pillow. From someone named X telling me he remembered what my parents smelled like when they burned. That we would be meeting again soon."

Those whispered words were broken glass as they came out of my mouth. And they hit Bastian as if I'd slapped him. His fingers didn't leave my hair, and his grip didn't tighten, but his face told me that I'd just wounded him worse than if I'd punched my fist into his chest and ripped his heart out. But I wasn't done, and he needed to know the rest.

"Emrys said that the note itself contained a blood curse—one that could take down entire families. She has no idea how I survived or why the curse's outcome is that I look like the Grim Reaper every few seconds. She's done everything she can think of to fix it, and she says she's researching, but..." I trailed off, shaking my head.

I was under pretty good authority that if Emrys hadn't found a way to fix it by now, there likely wasn't a fix to be had.

"And you kept this from me because?" he asked, the words hitting like a punch to the gut, even though they were gentle and soft and no more than a whisper.

How could I tell him that I worried he'd go off half-cocked and get himself killed? That if my parents couldn't save themselves from this X, what was he going to do? That I didn't trust him not to lock me down or keep me out of the fight, or not to run screaming away from the mere sight of me?

"You didn't want me to stop you. Is that it? You thought I would keep you from trying to find this bastard?"

I winced.

"Well, and Simon told me before all this about how

you ran screaming from the house when you met Isis."
I gestured to my face. "I kinda thought if you saw me
this way..." I didn't even attempt to continue. Just
saying it out loud made me realize how fucking dumb it
was.

Bastian and I didn't have this epic love affair. He
hadn't made me any promises or taken vows of forever.
We were tied tangentially by my need for blood and the
strange kind of possession I felt for him. But it didn't
ever feel like enough. The bond wasn't enough. The tie
we had to each other was fragile and fleeting.

And I didn't trust it.

That was the real reason I didn't tell him. Thomas
owed me. Emrys needed me. But Bastian... He could
leave me behind without a blink.

He nodded, his face grave as if he realized something
important. "You didn't trust me."

His face wavered as tears of shame filled my eyes,
and I couldn't hide because he was still cupping my
cheeks, making me face him. "No," I answered. "I
didn't."

His warm thumbs wiped the wetness away. "Do you
think you might someday? Trust me, I mean? If we had
more time?"

My chuckle was dark even as I covered both his
hands with my own, pressing them firmer into my skin.

"Everything I knew to be true was a lie. Everyone I knew deceived me. What does trust even mean?"

Bastian closed his eyes before resting his forehead against mine. "Trust means that you know I will be here to back you up when you need me. Trust means that I won't hide things from you or lie to you or hurt you on purpose. Trust means that you are safe with me. We haven't known each other long enough for you to believe me, I know that. All I'm asking is that you try. Because what I feel for you, I haven't felt in a very long time. I'm not ready to give that up."

In the circle of his arms with his heat radiating into me, I could almost taste the honesty on his tongue. He meant every single word he said.

"Okay," I murmured, doing my very best not to lie to him. "I'll try." These last few months had been hell, and I didn't think I could do another day of keeping him in the dark.

"Good. Now that I'm in the know, does that mean I might actually see you once in a while? Your absence is hell on a man's self-esteem."

I couldn't help the relieved laugh that burst from my lips. I also couldn't help that I launched myself at him, practically climbing his tall body like a tree and latching onto him as if he would disappear if I didn't wrap him up in my arms and legs as soon as possible.

I was a needy, needy barnacle.

Bastian's laugh was quickly swallowed by my kiss, and the joy in it was a welcome light when I'd been in the dark for so long. It didn't take long for that laugh to peter out or for him to realize that I meant business. Hell, if I could figure out how to manage it, I would have undressed him by the power of pent-up sexual frustration alone.

And when he finally figured out that I was serious? His gloriously strong hands gripped me tighter to him as if he wanted to fuse our skin. His whole body seemed to get warmer as he walked me backward to the closest wall. Then my fingers were under his shirt, exploring the planes of his stomach and higher.

That shirt really needed to go. Probably the pants, too.

When my thumb grazed a nipple, though, I suddenly found my hands out of his shirt and pinned above my head in his much larger one.

He broke the kiss, which ripped a groan from me. I wanted his lips back. I wanted the feel of his skin back. I wanted to fall into him, to roll around in his scent, in his touch until I was sated. Which might be never.

Bastian's green eyes flashed gold as air sawed in and out of his lungs. We were breathing as if we'd just ran for our lives, but Bastian's had the added flare of a man *this* close to coming undone.

"As much as I love where your head is at, I'm going to need you to stop, Sloane." His voice was pure gravel, and there was a slight manic quality to his expression, but I wouldn't be me without pressing my luck. So, naturally, I swiveled my hips—just a little—which made his eyes roll back in his head.

"Stop what?"

A growl ripped up his throat, and he nipped at my neck with his blunted teeth. *Dear sweet lord in heaven, why was that so fucking hot?* There was a solid threat of me combusting right then and there.

"Stop making me lose sense for about ten seconds, so I don't fuck you in a dirty, sticky bar. Let me take you home. Let me have you in a bed. Let me watch you writhe in my sheets as I taste you. Let me make lo—"

I cut him off with a kiss, his hands somehow no longer pinning mine. I was going to let him do all of that, but if he didn't stop talking about what he wanted to do to me, I'd be pushing the issue. Then we really would end up fucking against a wall in a deserted bar.

*Was it even deserted? Did it matter?*

"Okay," I managed to whisper once I broke our kiss. "Let's go home. And I'll let you do any filthy, dirty, nasty thing you want to me—sexually speaking—in the bed of your choosing. But I'm warning you…" I trailed off, giving my hips one more swivel just to see his gaze go molten.

"Warn me about what?"

I brought my lips right to his, so he could feel every word that came out of my mouth. "You're going to let me do everything I want to do to you, too. You're going to let me taste you, feel you, fuck you, make love to you." Evilly, I nipped at his bottom lip, which was swollen from all our kisses. "It's only fair."

Somehow, Bastian pressed himself further against me, and I felt every single millimeter of his arousal. Did my eyes roll up into my head? Maybe, but it was so hot to see him so close to losing it. I didn't know how in the hell I was supposed to handle it when his control finally snapped. But boy, did I want to be there when it did.

"Fair is fair, darling," he agreed, nodding to himself. He appeared as if he was shoving all of his lust into a little mental box to be opened at a later date. *Man, did I want to open that present.*

Then he stepped away from the wall, taking me with him. His grip didn't loosen one iota, but we were moving—and fast—like we were racing through time as everything around us sped up. The room, then the buildings and sky sped past us. Then we weren't in the club anymore. We were outside standing next to

Thomas' bike, which I'd parked nearly a mile away from my chosen rooftop.

The shock of the movement was probably the only thing that could have pulled me out of my lust haze.

"What the hell was that? How—"

"Mage trick," he muttered, letting me find my feet as he released me. "Let's just say that one isn't exactly aboveboard and may be illegal." He put a finger to his lips, signaling that I was to stay mum about it.

I snorted. Of course, he would use an illegal mage spell to get laid faster. To be honest, I couldn't exactly fault his logic.

"Sure you don't have any other tricks in your arsenal?" I teased, tossing my leg over the sleek motorcycle. "Can you make a portal to another dimension or conjure dark matter or something?" I shoved the black helmet on my head—not because I needed it, but so I didn't get pulled over.

Bastian just shrugged as if he could absolutely do those things if he put his mind to it, and it dawned on me that it was a distinct possibility that he wasn't joking.

"I'll meet you at the house," he said, dropping a kiss to my shoulder before nipping it with his teeth. "Be careful."

Every part of me clenched in answer, and I couldn't wait to feel his mouth on me again.

But as he stepped away, his phone buzzed in his pocket. Groaning, he fished it out and stared at the screen before his gaze immediately found mine.

I had a feeling I wouldn't be getting his mouth back for a very long time.

## 9

"Say that one more time?" I couldn't believe the bullshit I'd just heard, so there had to have been a mistake. There was no way that...

Bastian moved closer to me like he was going to have to lock me down. What he did not do was repeat himself, and I desperately needed him to.

"Is he—" I couldn't even say it.

His warm hands found my skin, but this time, they were too hot, too rough, too... "There was an attack on the Arcane Bureau of Investigation building in Knoxville tonight. Several agents are dead, and many are scattered to the winds. While that was going down, there was a prison break at our local detention facility. Booth escaped along with about twenty other prisoners. We need to get back to the house so we can help the ABI round up the fugitives."

I'd ripped my helmet off when he told me the first time, so I shoved it back on my head and started the bike. "I'll meet you there."

But before I could put it in gear and take off, Bastian had another too-hot hand on my bare arm. "We'll find him, Sloane."

I wanted to laugh, but I didn't. How many people would die because of that man? How many innocent people had died already? I wondered about the small dark-haired agent who'd given me advice. What had her name been? Sarina? Was she one of those dead agents? Was she hurt? She reminded me so much of Aunt Julie that my heart hurt to think about it.

Damn straight, we were going to find Booth. And this time, I wouldn't let a little thing like decorum stop me. Hell, I'd rip his soul right out of his body in front of a fucking audience if I had to. I'd known good and well I shouldn't have left him alive the last time, and what did I do? I let Emrys and Thomas talk me into being the good guy.

But I wasn't the good guy, and I never had been.

I gave Bastian a stiff nod and took off, letting the city lights race by me as I rocketed toward home.

The drive to the house had been too fast and not

fast enough. I wanted to get out there. I wanted to find Booth and tear his soul from his chest, and... Shaking my head, I ripped off the helmet and left it on the seat.

"What the fuck is wrong with your face?" a male voice yelled, scaring the shit out of me. "And why do you smell like death?"

Slowly, I turned to Simon, who was standing at the door to the garage with his skeleton kitty in his arms. Slapping at my chest, I tried to feel for my necklace. I wanted to roll my eyes but refrained. Bastian had taken my glamour necklace off of me, and it was undoubtedly still in his pocket.

Flannel shirt and haphazard beanie on his head, the tall death mage could likely scent the dead a mile away or something. Who knew what powers Simon had? From what I'd gleaned in my short time in this place, Simon and Bastian weren't exactly the norm when it came to their abilities.

"Is there a way we can just skip this whole conversation and pretend you didn't see anything?" I asked as I prayed Bastian got home with my necklace sometime in the next few seconds. The last thing I needed was the whole damn house up in my chili about my stupid face.

Simon stepped fully into the garage and shut the

door behind him. I had a feeling I knew what his answer was going to be.

"What in the bloody hell is going on, Sloane?" The threat in his tone was clear as day. He was going to get answers even if he had to pull them out of me with pliers.

Groaning, I eyed the giant bay door, hoping it would open so Bastian could explain to his brother why I looked like the Grim Reaper.

*No such luck.*

"Cliff's Notes? I touched a letter with a blood curse on it, and now I look like this. I swear I have a glamour, it's just in your brother's pocket. No big deal."

Simon gaped at me for a solid thirty seconds. I wasn't even sure he was breathing.

"Don't we have some fugitives to find?" I prompted, and the mention of our most pressing issue seemed to snap him out of it.

Simon's face took on an air of misery and commiseration. Hearing Booth was out in the world couldn't have been a comforting notion for him any more than it was for me. Not after Booth kidnapped him and tried to kill him to draw me out. Or at least that's what I figured the motive had been. It didn't matter how much blood I'd pulled from Booth during his interrogation. I'd gleaned a slight bit more than fuck all from him.

A part of me wondered if Simon blamed me for his ordeal. It wasn't exactly as if I'd been around in the last couple of months to see if he held a grudge or anything.

"Does Emrys know?" he whispered, and I nodded, which made him breathe a sigh of relief. "And Thomas?"

I nodded again.

"Bastian?"

"He found out tonight. He wasn't keeping it from you or anything."

Simon dipped his head, a frown marring his face before he set his skeleton kitty down. I'd avoided Isis—and damn near everyone else in the house—for months. I wasn't exactly skipping to find out if she would freak out around me now. The last time she'd accidentally wandered too close to Clementine—our resident revenant—there had been several knocked-over vases that paid the price.

But I probably shouldn't have worried. Isis and I were tight. Ever since I'd come to the house, she had taken a keen interest in me, much to Simon's dismay. Isis raced for me, leaping in the air once she got close enough and damn near landing on my chest. My arms closed around her kitty butt, gentle, so I didn't hurt her. Immediately, she started purring as if I was her favorite person on the planet as she rubbed her boney head against my cheek.

Simon's frown intensified, the concern on his face making me a little uneasy. "You know, you're the only person she does that to. She hates Thomas, Axel, and Clem because they're undead. She can't stand Harper or Emrys—something about their magic she doesn't like. She tolerates Dahlia, but only because Dahlia is around her so much. Other than me, Isis is not a fan of almost anyone. Except you."

I shrugged around an armful of kitty, wondering if anyone had told him about just how close Isis and I were. She was the one to show me the way when he'd been taken. Isis was the one who had made sure I knew where he was. She had comforted me when I'd learned of Aunt Julie's death, and cuddling this tiny creature, I felt a relief I usually only got in Bastian's arms.

"You said it was a blood curse? That made you this way? A killing curse, I presume?" Simon edged toward me. An understanding dawned on his face, and he pulled in the air with his nose, scenting me.

I cuddled Isis closer, the urge to run away from Simon flitting through my bones.

"Do you know who death mages make deals with? Who we call upon to do our magic?" Simon asked, a prompt that felt like a trap.

I shook my head, taking a step backward. "No, I don't."

"I didn't either for a very long time. It wasn't until I was well advanced, did I learn the truth about what we do. Everything a death mage does is a trade. A deal. A bargain." With every sentence, Simon moved toward me.

The urge to run grew stronger because I knew he was about to drop a bomb on me—a truth I was positive I was in no way ready for.

"We make the bargains with a deity. He goes by many names in many cultures. But the most common of names is the Angel of Death."

The sound of that name sent a pang of alarm through me for no good reason whatsoever. I didn't want to know this—didn't want whatever he was going to say in my brain.

"That's great information, Simon. Why the fuck are you telling me this?" Reluctantly, I set Isis on her feet, getting ready to make a break for it if I had to. "No offense, but I was under the impression we had shit to do that didn't involve story time about death deities."

Luckily, my reprieve came in the form of Bastian pulling into the open bay door, the headlights of the SUV temporarily blinding me.

"We will be continuing this conversation, dammit,"

Simon whispered, less like he was talking to me and more like he was talking to himself. Still, I heard him.

Bastian threw the SUV into park and hopped out. Well, it was less hop and more of a sexy step out, but whatever. His gaze found mine, concern stamped all over his face before his eyes cut to his brother. Without a word, Bastian invaded my space, moving in front of me in a protective stance between his brother and me. It wasn't until his big body was between Simon and me that I realized just how close Simon had been.

"Do we have a problem?" Bastian asked, his voice calm and level as if he was discussing the weather. I couldn't tell if he was actually pissed or not, but I in no way wanted to be a sticking point between the brothers.

"There's no problem," I answered, pivoting so I was no longer behind Bastian. "Can I have my necklace back? I'd rather not freak out anyone else tonight."

Bastian peeled his gaze from his brotherly staring match to look at me. Instantly, his face softened a bit. He held out his hand, my necklace dangling from his fingers as if he'd been holding it the whole time. My fingertips brushed his skin as I plucked the necklace from his hand, and even with the knowledge that Booth was out there, that we had work to do, that his brother was standing less than three feet from us, it was as if there was no one else on the planet.

"Excuse me," Simon said, his plaintive barb shattering our tiny moment of peace. "You're just okay with this?" He gestured to my face, and it stung a little that he was being so damn rude.

Okay, it stung a lot.

I fell back a step, quickly fastening the pendant around my neck. If that's how he was going to be, then fine. I could see the writing on the wall. I moved for the garage door that led to the main house.

"Just shut up, Simon," Bastian growled, his innate need to stick up for me softening Simon's blow.

"No, that's not—" Simon began, but I heard a thud, and Bastian cut him off.

I couldn't help but glance back. Simon now had a bloody nose, and Bastian appeared as if he was gearing up to hit him again.

"Shut. Up." Bastian's finger was in Simon's face, the tip lit with crackling magic.

Simon's eyes were pleading, his hands up in surrender. "But—"

"I swear to everything holy," Bastian snarled in his brother's face, "if you say another fucking word, I'm going to make you wish you were never born."

"What's the meaning of this?" Emrys' Irish lilt broke the silence, making all of us whip to attention like good little soldiers.

Simon's chuckle was only slightly nervous, but he answered for us all. "Just a brotherly tiff, Em. Nothing to worry about. You know how it is."

He offered her a shrug that said, "What are you gonna do?" and skirted around his brother to the door. Emrys' gaze narrowed on Bastian and me as if we were the troublemakers of the group. I knew I was, but Bastian was practically a choir boy. Sorta.

"We have a job to do. I suggest you save all tiffs until it's over."

Sound advice.

If only there wasn't this feeling in my gut that whatever Simon wanted to tell me was something I really needed to know.

## 10

"I want you with Thomas," Emrys ordered as she loaded her belt with potion bottles and other various weapons.

She had been pairing me with Thomas for the last two months, and it was fine before. But now that Bastian knew about me, the urge to have him close by while we were in danger was something of a need of mine.

I opened my mouth to protest, but one look from her odd reddish eyes and I snapped my trap shut.

"And you aren't going after Booth."

That got it open again. "What? You're out of your mind if you thin—"

Emrys shifted her weight, her irises getting the odd glow they got when she was about to zap something to kingdom come. "The pair of you are going after higher-value targets. The ones we cannot afford to lose. As much of a murderer as Booth McCall is, he is not the worst of the worst. I need my strongest hitters out there to find them. A shifter is not my highest priority."

True, Booth was just a shifter, but he had information. He knew who X was. I could feel it. He knew the arcaner who'd killed my parents. His sins were mine to have, mine to take. His soul was mine.

"Who's going after him then?" I challenged, likely to my own detriment.

An evil smile curled the edges of her mouth. "I will. Bastian, Simon, and I will be going after the mid-level targets. Axel and Dahlia will be assisting you and Thomas. Harper and Clem will be staying put. Any other questions about my logistical prowess, or can I continue preparing myself?"

I didn't like any of this. I was being sidelined—big time.

"Be sure to collect extra weapons from Clementine before you go and an earpiece from Harper. Thomas has your assigned targets."

And now I was being shoved off, shooed away like an annoying gnat.

"They know—Bastian and Simon—about this." I

gestured to my face, moving my index finger all the way around my mug for "extra" emphasis. "Bastian knows about the note as well." I couldn't say why those words felt like a threat, but they really did. If she was going to shoo me away, I was going to metaphorically flip her off before I left.

Yeah, it was childish, but dammit, compared to everyone else in the house, I *was* the child.

Without another word, I left her with that information and made my way to Clem.

But before I could get to the undead de facto housekeeper, cook, and weapons keeper of the Night Watch, I was waylaid by a tiny, permanently angry empath.

"What the hell is going on with you?" Harper griped, nearly scaring the life out of me. She must have snuck up behind me as I debated the merits of searching for Booth myself.

Turning, I only managed to blink at her. Did she really need me to spell it out?

"Well, Harper, when the man who murdered your last living family breaks out of prison—"

Harper rolled her eyes at me. "That's not what I mean. Your warding is all..." She paused to gesture at the whole of my person. "Off. It's fine right now, but every once in a while, I get a wave of bullshit from you.

And then..." She snapped her fingers. "Nothing. What—and I cannot stress this enough—the fuck?"

I was already done with this conversation. Pinching the bridge of my nose, I sighed. "I have no idea. It's not like I can do my own warding. I'll ask Emrys if she can fix it."

"You'd better," she grumped, crossing her arms over her chest.

That's when I finally noticed the fear she was trying so desperately to hide.

"You okay?" I asked, wondering if anyone thought to ask her that. As the resident hermit, Harper rarely ventured out of her rooms, preferring the company of computers to anything living. As an empath, Harper might feel trapped in a house like this—unable to go outside for fear of what she might feel from others. Then again, this might be her one safe spot.

"I'm *fine*," she huffed. "I mean, it's not as if he was my friend or anything. It's not as if we hadn't spent years getting to know each other only for him to betray us all. It's not as if—" She shook her head, turning away from me like just looking at me hurt her. "I know it's selfish. I know what you lost. I know what I'm going through doesn't matter. It's just..."

Under normal circumstances, I'd give someone dealing with this level of bullshit a hug. But touching

Harper wasn't ever going to be an option. "It's okay to feel what you feel. There isn't a right way or a wrong way. And I'm sorry that you lost a friend."

"It makes me want all the wards down, you know," she muttered, still facing away. "Even if that means I'll go crazy."

Before I could formulate a response to that, she was gone, stalking off toward her rooms and leaving me behind.

"Are you fucking shitting me?" I growled, chasing a sorcerer up a ladder. This particular ladder led to the tippy top of a water tower that had to be five if not ten stories tall. I was not a fan of heights. I also was not a fan of falling off of said heights.

Landings hurt—a lot.

This particular sorcerer was the last target on our list and a certified pain in my ass. Of the ten arcaners we'd bagged and tagged, this guy was the fucking worst. The first nine hadn't precisely been picnics, but this guy?

It was bad enough that I'd been chasing him for the last twenty-four hours on no sleep, no blood, and no food. But he could do a weird little portal jump thing that made catching the fucker an actual problem. One second, he'd be one place, and the next, he'd be fifty feet away. And he was fast, the spell work or ability or whatever was something he could just do, quick as a whip. I figured he'd tire out eventually, but so far, his energy had seemed endless.

And why was I the one chasing him up a water tower? Oh, it was because this bastard had volleyed spells at us, one after the other, until he managed to hit something. Thomas was somewhere behind me healing from an acid bomb, and Axel was still recovering from an explosion of knifelike barbs that hit him square in the chest. Good thing this sorcerer's aim wasn't better, or Axel would be missing a head and really, really dead.

I was the only one left standing, and it was the principle of the thing at this point. As soon as I caught this bastard, I would be breaking every single bone in his hands and feet before using my last stasis potion.

The hunt prior to this had been almost too easy—especially when compared to this asshole. The detention center and ABI had blood samples from every inmate that made locator spells a breeze. Dahlia found them and spelled Thomas' GPS app to update on their locations as they moved. It was like shooting fish in a barrel… if that barrel was filled with piranhas. All we needed to do was ambush the fugitives and hit them with a stasis spell.

Our only problem was the portal jumper who—no matter how good my aim was—I couldn't hit.

But for the last five minutes, he hadn't jumped through any portals. I hoped he was—*finally*—petering out. I needed food and a bed and not to be chasing this damn sorcerer all over the ass-end of Tennessee.

When I was close to the top catwalk, I smartly—or at least I thought it was smart—ducked. The last thing I needed was to lose my head in the literal sense. A flash of heat skimmed my shoulder, the searing magic burning right through my suit to my skin. The orange jump-suited sorcerer had finally tagged me. Growling, I launched myself the last few feet up the ladder, landing on the catwalk right next to him.

The scraggly-looking man was probably older than dirt but didn't show it. With matted dark hair and wild blue eyes, he stared at me as if I was the boogeyman. His dirt-encrusted fingers weaved more magic, but I refused to get hit with anything else. Before he could complete another spell—or jump for that matter—I caught the side of his face in my hand and bounced his head off the side of the water tower. The sound of his skull making impact was the best thing I'd heard in two damn days.

*Let's see you do spells unconscious, you bastard.*

My satisfaction ramped up another notch when I poured the stasis potion over his still form. The milky-white liquid snaked around his body, binding his arms and legs together. It also had the added benefit of making it so he couldn't do any magic of any kind or wake up until he got the counter-potion.

*Take that, you fuck.*

And that was around the time that I realized I was at the top of a water tower with an unconscious prisoner that I needed to haul to the ground.

By myself.

*Super.*

I was tempted to just sit down until Thomas or Axel or hell, even Dahlia found us. I did not want to shlep this asshole back down the ladder, and I sure as hell didn't want to accidentally drop him, or fall, or... I made the mistake of looking down and had to hold back bile as I scrambled away from the railing.

Yeah, there was no way I was going to be able to do that. I would just have to live up here until the world ended or this water tower collapsed—whichever came first. My legs gave a slight wobble, and I found myself on my ass on the metal catwalk.

Two thuds not only scared the shit out of me, but they also seemed to rock the whole damn tower.

"What, you just going to sit there?" Axel teased, his Texan accent softening the blow of his words, but only a little. Still, the likely harmless taunt grated my last nerve.

*Bravado. I would go with bravado.* "I didn't see you bagging anyone. Just because I'm having an internal logistical deliberation does not mean that I was resting."

Axel snorted, putting his hands on his jean-clad hips. "Is that what they're calling panic attacks these days? Weird."

I studied his battered cowboy boots, not meeting his gaze. Only Axel would be hunting monster fugitives in western-style boots. "Oh, fuck you."

"Yeah, yeah. That's what all the ladies say."

The man knelt next to me, but I still refused to turn my head. Doing that meant looking out. And looking out meant looking down. Hard pass.

"Now, do you want me to get the perp or you first?"

The question was kind, but I still hated that it had to be asked. And since I had a death grip on the metal grating of the catwalk and likely wouldn't be able to let it go anytime soon, I jutted my chin at the sorcerer.

"Take him. I need a minute."

I needed a crowbar and a sedative, but whatever.

Axel hauled the sorcerer onto his shoulder like he was picking up a bag of feed or something and just freaking jumped. Here I was, trying to even contemplate the *possibility* of getting down and Axel just. Fucking.

Jumped off the side of the tower like the landing wouldn't crush an average person.

Another thud of feet landing right next to me had me squeaking like a mouse.

"Am I going to have to blindfold you?" Thomas needled, kneeling at my left.

*Asshole.*

I might not have been able to look at Axel, but Thomas was close enough that looking at him didn't mean staring out at the horizon. I shot him a scathing glare and was tempted to flip him off for good measure, but I never got the chance. Before I knew it, I was up and over Thomas' shoulder in a fireman's carry, and then he was jumping off the tower just like Axel had.

I didn't even get the chance to scream.

I did, however, get the chance to vomit on his boots once we landed, so, there was that.

## 11

By the time we got to the ABI detention center, I hadn't quite managed to forgive Thomas for launching me off the tower. Thomas was still in the process of forgiving Axel and Dahlia, who laughed so hard at my up-chuck episode they were rolling on the ground. He'd already told me he would forgive me around about never.

"I didn't see you puking on Bastian when he did it to you," Thomas grumbled for the fifth time as he threw the truck in park. For this mission, we used the giant truck that usually took up residence in the last bay of the garage. The king cab was roomy enough for the four of us, and the extended bed with the shell, made transporting ten immobile fugitives a breeze. We'd had to pass three different checkpoints just to get this far, and I was over all of this rigamarole.

Axel chuckled before socking Thomas in the arm. "That's because she doesn't want to kiss you, dummy. If she did, I suspect she'd be too busy swooning to puke on your shoes."

"Fuck off, Axel," Thomas and I said at the same time. We'd done this at least three times on the four-hour drive from the east ass-end of nowhere Tennessee to the outskirts of Knoxville. But I figured it was because no one had gotten a lick of rest or sleep since the day before last. How we were still awake was a freaking mystery, and I was not handling the lack of sleep very well.

"Please tell me the processing is going to be a snap because I can't take much more of this," Dahlia said, her husky voice laced with sleepy irritation.

"My question is—why are we taking them back to the prison they escaped from?" Axel complained, staring out the windshield at the approaching guards. "Isn't that like putting a bird back in a broken cage?"

He wasn't wrong, but right now, I just did not give that first shit. I wanted these prisoners out of this truck and to be someone else's problem—at least for the next twenty-four hours.

A very tall woman knocked on Thomas' window, the rap of her knuckles practically shaking the whole truck.

She had dark hair tied back from her tan face, the braids and dreads a serious complement to her Viking-like appearance. Thomas rolled down the window, ready to speak to the giant woman, but she wasn't looking at him.

No, the very tall, very intimidating prison guard was staring right at me.

Piercing green eyes assessed me as she held her hand out to Thomas for the paperwork. He produced the bounty contracts, and she snatched them out of his hand, never moving her gaze from mine.

I wanted to sink into my seat or turn into a slug or something just to get this woman to stop staring at me. Did I have "criminal" tattooed on my forehead or something?

"Everyone out of the vehicle," she barked and took a few steps back so Thomas could exit his door.

Reluctantly, I followed suit, my tired body revolting at the thought of standing. My feet yowled at me as I made contact with the pavement, but I refused to let this woman see me wince.

Only when I was out of the relative safety of the vehicle did she take her gaze off me and inspect the paperwork. "Twenty fugitives in two days. I have to say, I'm impressed. Only one left on the list. A Booth McCall?"

Thomas shifted forward, his economy of movement putting him between the guard and me, but it was Axel who answered her. His Southern charm was in full force as he reached for her hand. "Yes, ma'am. Our other team is busy rounding him up. Shouldn't be too long now."

The guard nodded, still looking at the paperwork. "A few of these boys were coded 'dead or alive.' You didn't bring me any stiffs, did you?"

Axel chuckled, hooking his thumbs through his belt loops as he seemed to relax. "No, ma'am, we did not. Captured them all alive. They're in a stasis spell, and some of them are a little roughed up, but everybody's breathing."

The guard glanced up then, assessing Axel. In flat boots, the pair of them were eye to eye, and the guard noticed it, too. A faint blush rose in her cheeks as Axel gave her a big old grin. The curvy, giant of a guard was ridiculously pretty with high cheekbones and a pouty lip. If it didn't look as if she could break me in two, I was sure we'd be besties.

"Is that so?"

We had now entered the flirting portion of today's activities, but as long as the armed prison guard wasn't staring at me like she wanted to murder me, I was all for it.

"I have the counter-potions to remove their stasis,"

Dahlia suggested, breaking the flirty spell Axel had on the guard.

She blinked hard at Axel for a second before moving her stern gaze to Dahlia. The small witch offered her a velvet bag full of clinking spell bottles. The guard accepted them, nodding as if this was all procedure or something. "I'll ask you to offload the prisoners to the steps. Once we have confirmed identity, we will accept them and cut you the remittance."

Dahlia gave the tall guard a smile. "No problem."

Without much prompting, I hauled my butt to the back of the truck and started yanking on feet. The sooner these guys were back in jail, the sooner I could go to sleep. If I could even sleep.

*You heard what she said. They haven't caught him yet. Booth is still out there.*

A shiver of unease raced through me, a worry that hadn't been able to take root before. I'd been running my ass off for two days, and all the while, I hadn't spoken to Bastian. As far as I knew, none of us had heard from Bastian, Simon, or Emrys at all.

Thomas and Axel met me at the back of the truck, helping me remove the frozen prisoners from the vehicle.

I wanted to ask, but I just couldn't. It made sense that we hadn't heard from them. They were chasing a shifter through who knew where. A man that could change into any animal at will. I wondered how that stacked up to the portal-jumper and had to admit to myself that their job was likely more complicated by far.

It didn't take long to deposit the prisoners on the steps of the detention center. The giant gray building gave me the major creeps. It resembled an abandoned asylum right out of an awful horror movie. I couldn't even imagine going inside. Asylums made me think of dead people, which made me think of ghosts, which gave me the ultimate heebies.

Bad guys in need of killing? *Sign me up.*

Ghosts? *No, thank you.*

The giant guard barked out a laugh for what seemed like no good reason, pulling my attention to her. She met my gaze and shook her head, giving me a smile for the first time.

At my quizzical expression, she approached, her demeanor considerably less hostile than it had been just five minutes prior. "Sorry about all that. It's just—" She shook her head as if she were debating with herself. "You're wearing a glamour," she muttered under her breath, sotto voce as if this information was just between us.

I took a step away from her, my attention shifting to the checkpoints that I knew I had no shot in hell of getting through in one piece. I was not walking into that prison if I could help it. Only the first couple of gunshots stung, right?

"No, no. Don't worry. It's not a crime to wear a glamour. A lot of arcaners do it if they can't pass as human. But with the prison break and everything, we're all a little on edge." Her lips twisted as her internal debate continued. "Your friends are okay. A little banged up, but nothing a good night's sleep won't cure."

I frowned, shifting my gaze to Thomas.

"No, not him. Your boyfriend and his brother and your boss," she said, making me whip around to face her.

I took a real step back then.

She rolled her eyes and shook her head, seemingly exasperated at herself. She thrust out a hand. "I'm Siobhan Byrne. Psychic, medium, intuitive, whatever. I apologize for overstepping. You just seemed worried about your people, is all."

Reluctantly, I took her offered hand. "Sloane Cabot."

Her giant palm engulfed mine. "Pleased to meet you." But when our skin touched, her pupils dilated for a second as a frown creased her brow. "They'll find him soon, but he isn't the one you seek. Change is coming. Death too. Death is looking for you."

I wanted to move—really, I did—but I just couldn't.

Not only was my hand lost in hers, but Siobhan's grip was so tight it was cutting off all the blood to my fingers.

"Death will find you again," she said, her voice taking on a monotone quality that gave me the fucking creeps. "He will find you like the flames found your parents."

Shock pumped ice water through my veins. What the hell did she know about my parents? Siobhan let out a shuddering groan like she was in agony, and to my utter surprise, her grip got even tighter. My fingers felt like they were being crushed under the weight of whatever she was seeing.

And then my hand wasn't trapped anymore. It wasn't trapped because Axel, Thomas, and Dahlia were now in between me and Siobhan, and the giant guard was clutching her head.

"I think it's time to go, don't you?" Thomas muttered, ushering me into the back seat of the truck.

My steps were wooden as I followed his prodding direction, my feelings, my thoughts, all of it on pause as he dutifully buckled me in like a toddler. He then shut my door, climbed into the driver seat, and started the truck.

"You okay?" Thomas asked, his voice a gentle

reminder that my emotions should be lambasting my psyche right about now.

I met his gaze in the rearview mirror, and he winced at what he saw there.

"Is she right?" I croaked, the pain starting to bubble up inside me. I couldn't foresee a time in my life when the mention of their deaths would be anything less than the worst sort of torture.

Thomas shook his head. "I don't know."

*That was what I was afraid he'd say.*

"You're staying here, and I don't want to hear a word about it. Don't make me make Axel sedate you."

I fought off the urge to flip Thomas off and sneak out, but I was under no illusion that he hadn't already thought of that. I tried not to be put out that Thomas sidelined me for the rest of the mission. No one thought letting me search for Booth was a good idea. I had no doubt it was because if I found him, he wouldn't be going back to the ABI detention center alive. Evidently, Booth had been coded as an "alive only" bounty, just like I had once upon a time.

Thomas and Dahlia had wolfed down a quick meal before heading back out, but Axel and I were told to stay put. I had a feeling Axel's new mission was to babysit me. Rather than get too butthurt about it, I decided to take a shower, get some food, and attempt to sleep, worry for Bastian and Simon making that task seem almost impossible.

I knew I wouldn't be able to get any rest, and it didn't matter if I'd been running for two straight days. But as exhausted as I was, sleep snared me without too much effort on my part, the rest fitful and full of dark things.

Screams.

Fire.

I kept waking up, but sleep clawed at me, trapping me again and again until its hold was too strong for me to break.

*My mother was screaming at me, pressing on my chest over and over again. Her hands were hard, weighty like they were fifty-pound dumbbells just chilling on my ribcage. I wanted to answer her, but I just couldn't. Everything hurt. Everything. From my toes all the way up to my hair, every single bit of me felt as if I was being flash fried by a blowtorch, followed by an acid bath.*

*I couldn't understand her words, either. I was either going deaf or she was speaking gibberish, and I was in so much pain it really didn't matter. It didn't matter when the agony made me want to die.*

*The room around us was hazy at best. Smoke swirled and*

*bloomed in a halo around her head as an odd purple light whirled up her arms. And she was crying. Or at least I thought she was. A tiny trail of a tear dropped from her eye and hit me on the cheek. I wanted to wipe it away. Wanted to tell her I was okay— I wasn't—but I couldn't do that, either.*

*Her strong fingers gripped my shoulders, and she pulled me into her arms, hugging me to her chest as if she was saying goodbye.*

*That's when I saw the flames.*

*That's when I saw my dad lying in a pool of his own blood in the middle of the living room.*

*That's when I saw the man in the gray suit, his face shrouded within the shadows, kneeling over my father.*

*He held a wicked-looking knife in his hand—bigger than a dagger but smaller than a sword—the awful blade coated in my father's blood. He rose from his crouch, an awful laugh bubbling up his throat as the sound danced over the roar of the flames and my mother's sobs.*

*And he was coming for us.*

The trill of a cell phone had me gasping for breath as I shot out of bed like the hounds of Hell were on my ass. I knew the phone had been what woke me up, and I was grateful for the tiny device. The smell of smoke was in my nose, a leftover echo of a dream that was quickly fading from my brain.

I wanted to hold onto it, clutch it in my hand so I

could mine it for clues, but the damn thing seemed to be no more tangible than smoke and twice as slippery.

The phone stopped ringing only to begin again, the Night-Watch-issued cell phone blaring an old Deftones song. Groggily, I picked it up, spying Bastian's name on the screen before I answered it.

"Sloane?" Bastian's voice filled my ear, and I breathed the biggest sigh of relief ever.

"Are you okay?" I began, the worry snaking up my throat.

*Of course he's fine, Sloane. He wouldn't be calling if he was dead.*

"I'm fine, but I need you to get over here." His tone was wary, as if he didn't want to tell me whatever it was he was going to say next.

"Over where?" I held the phone in between my cheek and shoulder as I plucked my pants from the floor and yanked them on.

"Whispering Pines Cemetery," he said, the quiet words hitting me like a haymaker to the chest.

And then he dropped the mother of all bombs.

"We found Booth."

usk was falling as I dismounted Thomas'
bike in the tiny parking lot of Whispering
Pines Cemetery. A year ago, I'd woken up in
this very graveyard with no memory of how or why I
ended up here. Honestly, it still didn't make sense
to me.

I doubted it ever would.

The gate to the cemetery was open a crack, the
wrought iron creaking back and forth in the slight
breeze, the scent of death cloying on the air. Bastian had
told me there was no rush. To be careful. But I'd thrown
on the first pieces of clothing I could get my hands on
and hauled ass to my small hometown.

But as much as I wanted to be sure that Booth was
taken down, I had a hell of a time convincing myself to

walk through that gate. My hesitation didn't make much sense either. I'd been to this cemetery a hundred times, burying bad guys that were too young to turn to ash. I knew the groundskeeper personally—or as personally as one could know the guy they were bribing to keep his trap shut.

*One foot in front of the other, Sloane. Keep moving.*

My mother's words often came to me in times like this. Times I didn't want to do the hard thing—and make no mistake, this was going to be a hard thing. I followed her sage advice, ripping the helmet off my head and setting it on the seat before marching toward the gate.

The scent that merely tickled my nose before, now hit me with the force of a battering ram.

Sweeping my gaze over the familiar headstones, my eyes immediately went in the direction of my parents' graves. It didn't matter how many times I'd been here, I always looked there first. Plus, the awful aroma was practically a neon sign pointing the way. I saw Bastian before anyone else, the tall man refusing to blend in with the monuments and headstones. Next to him were his brother and our boss, and beside her was the famed groundskeeper, Gerry. Gerry and Emrys were slightly off to the side, discussing something I couldn't hear, but that wasn't what gave me pause.

Gerry's and Emrys' body language were of two people who knew each other—were friends even. And I likely would have focused on that new bit of information had my advancing steps not brought Booth into view.

Or what was left of him.

Bastian hadn't told me Booth was dead on the phone. Sure, I'd assumed that was the case when he'd insisted that the rush wasn't necessary, but this was...

"What the hell did you do?" I accused. The words were meant to be under my breath, but they cracked like a whip through the quiet night.

I didn't know who exactly I was accusing either, but good fucking god, this man was... Bile crept up my throat, and I had to turn away. I'd seen some awful things in the last year. But what was done to Booth? It was a thing of nightmares.

And I didn't know if I was pissed he'd been killed before I'd gotten my answers, or that I hadn't been the one to do it.

"We didn't do this," Bastian said, his warmth and voice right next to me, seeping into my space like a welcome weight. "Gerry found him like this when he arrived and called us straightaway."

Ah, the aforementioned Gerry. It was a curious thing that Gerry of all people knew to call the Night Watch about what had to have been a ritualistic murder. I couldn't imagine the local cops dealing with this mess. Just from the small glimpse I'd gotten, I knew that Booth was in pieces.

Lots and lots of pieces.

"And he knew to call you because?"

Already I was putting two and two together. A few months ago, Gerry had given me a stern warning about the arcane world finding out about my little hobby. The very next night I'd been ambushed by Bastian himself. It didn't take a genius to figure out that Gerry had ratted me out.

*See if I ever buy him whiskey again, the lush.*

Bastian sighed. "He keeps us in the loop occasionally. Whispering Pines doesn't have a large arcane population, but Gerry hears things. He's been helpful."

I snorted, refusing to turn to face Bastian. "A tattletale is more like it. He have a reason why the cops aren't here already? Whispering Pines didn't get its name for being a raucous kind of place. Whatever was done to Booth would have caused a stir."

Stir was putting it mildly.

Shuddering, I tried to scrub my brain of the images dancing at the forefront of my mind, but it was impossible. The slight breeze turned into a gust, bombarding me with the heavy scent of decaying blood, bile, excrement, urine, and all the rest of the awful smells a body produced in the throes of death.

"Harper checked for us. There haven't been any calls about a disturbance. Either he was unconscious—which I fucking well hope so—or whoever did this cast a spell so no one heard."

Personally, I didn't hope Booth was unconscious when he died, but that was just me. Booth McCall had taken the last of my loved ones from me. I hoped he felt every cut. For what he'd done to Julie, he deserved it.

Booth seemed to have been cut into sections—hands, elbows shoulders, feet, knees, hips. The scent of the blood drying on the grass meant that this had to have been done while he was still breathing. But first, he'd been skinned.

And he hadn't been dumped here. Oh, no.

Booth had been meticulously dismembered while he was still alive, his shifter abilities likely prolonging the torture. The only part of him untouched was his head, which rested against a rather familiar headstone.

It should be familiar. It had my damn name on it.

"Do you figure him being on my grave is a message, a gift, or a warning?" I asked conversationally, as if it wasn't a huge deal that the man to steal so much from me was laid out on my grave like a sacrifice.

Moreover, I wondered if X knew I was still alive—if

he knew that his blood curse didn't kill me. I wondered if he put Booth on my grave as a taunt. Honestly, it wouldn't surprise me.

Bastian sighed deep enough that it sounded as if his soul was escaping his body.

"To be honest?" Simon said, startling me almost out of my boots. "I'm a bit more worried about the magic used to perform the task than the message. Did you see those sigils?"

Where the hell had he come from? And how had he so soundlessly approached?

Simon gave the pair of us a wide smile, as if startling me was his end goal. *Dick.*

"Don't do that," Bastian chided. "You know shade jumping to eavesdrop is just rude."

*Shade jumping?*

Simon appeared affronted. "I wasn't eavesdropping. I was listening to a conversation that had to do with the topic at hand."

Bastian rolled his eyes at his little brother. "That you weren't a member of."

"Sigils? I don't remember seeing any sigils. Then again, I was probably too focused on the dead body on my grave."

Simon gave me a solemn nod. "No way was any of

this done by hand. The whole place smells of dark magic."

Funny, I couldn't smell anything over the blood.

"Only you can smell that, Simon. Trust me." I shuddered, the scent of Booth's death grating on my brain enough for me to move upwind. Only, when I got closer to Emrys and Gerry—who were still in their familiar huddle—I could sense what Simon had been talking about. It had me wishing I hadn't moved. I'd take the scent of Booth's death over this.

Gagging, I nearly ran away from the scene as I headed for Gerry's office. It smelled of rotting things, dead things. Dark things.

"See," Simon said behind me, the brothers hot on my heels as I sought refuge and air. "Like I said. Dark magic."

Emerging from the groundskeeper's office, Thomas and Dahlia intercepted our little group, preventing my escape. Thomas shook his head at someone over my shoulder—either Bastian or Simon—I couldn't tell which. Honestly, I didn't really care. I needed untainted air and now.

Skirting around Thomas, I marched right for Gerry's office, heading for the bottle of whiskey I knew was stashed in his bottom desk drawer under old rags.

Maybe the alcohol would singe my nostrils enough to wash that smell out.

Thomas and Bastian were muttering behind me about something, but I blocked out their voices in favor of my search of alcohol. I located the bottle—nearly three-quarters gone—and cracked the lid. If I chugged the rest, it would be just desserts for the little tattletale.

"She smelled it, didn't she?" Thomas asked, as if me smelling magic was something new.

I swallowed the decidedly cheap whiskey, the burn of it doing the trick of making that smell go away—at least for a little while. "Of course I did. It was like rotting things and..."

A shudder racked my whole body, making the hairs on my arms stand on end. I needed a shower and a blowtorch for my olfactory glands.

"Only magic-users can smell that, Sloane," Thomas instructed, and if he hadn't said it with such condescending conviction, I probably wouldn't have been so irritated.

I rolled my eyes before casting them in Bastian's direction. "Really?"

"Really," Thomas answered for him. "I can't scent what you're describing. I only smell death and blood."

I tried to recall if this was a new trait for me or if I'd had it this past year. I couldn't remember if I'd just scented the ozone of spent magic or the spells themselves, but figured it wasn't that big of a deal. So I could smell this magic? So what? "We all know I'm a freak, Thomas. That isn't exactly new information."

He huffed. "No, but being able to scent out an incredibly rare mind-bendingly complicated kind of magic is. Especially when most arcaners can't."

"I can't smell it, either," Dahlia offered. "But I blame that on my diluted genes and less on you being a magical bloodhound."

At least someone was talking sense. "Oh, what difference does it make?"

Being able to smell the magic that tore Booth apart wouldn't help me find X. It wouldn't help me learn how he'd killed my parents. And who gave a fuck how and why Booth died? It wasn't rocket science. Booth knew shit he probably shouldn't, and now he was dead. This X likely killed him to keep his mouth shut.

It wasn't as if I'd be able to go door-to-door to sniff people to find the elusive X, either. I'd scoured Ascension, Knoxville, Whispering Pines, and everywhere else I could think of for clues. X was a fucking ghost, and being able to smell the magic he used to murder his loose end wasn't going to change that.

But I couldn't say that out loud.

Booth had been with these people for a long time

before I got here. He was their friend, their family, and he'd betrayed them. I was the physical embodiment of his betrayal. I was the giant elephant in the room that no one wanted to talk about, and if I told them just how much I didn't give a shit about Booth's death, well...

That would make me heartless, now, wouldn't it?

Maybe I *was* heartless—an unfeeling monster with no remorse.

But just maybe, that was what was necessary to get shit done.

The group of them talked amongst themselves for a bit while I downed the rest of Gerry's whiskey. The swill wasn't quite doing the trick anymore, and all too quickly it was gone. Simon and Thomas were still discussing my wonder nose, and I'd parked my ass on Gerry's desk, purposefully messing up the papers there with my ass.

Granted, Gerry had likely done me a favor in ratting me out. I had food in my belly, a roof over my head, and —dare I say it—friends. Still, snitches got stitches and all that.

"Do you know how rare that magic is?" Simon shouted, throwing his hands up. He was probably talking to me, but he wasn't looking at me. He was looking at Bastian, stabbing his finger in his big brother's sternum to hammer home his point. "It's outlawed death magic from the Byzantine Era. There are no books about it. The only way to learn it is from someone who already knew it, and it's damn near impossible to teach. The only way to detect it is if you're a death mage." He gestured to himself with both his thumbs. "*Or—*"

"We fucking talked about this, Simon," Bastian growled, cutting him off and stepping closer to his brother.

Simon's face reddened, and he appeared to be about a millisecond from hauling back and socking Bastian a good one.

"Oh, would you two work out your shit already?" Thomas griped, plopping down on the desk right next to me. "ABI buildings getting raided. Prison breaks. I just got a call an hour ago from my old nest. They got attacked by a bunch of unnested vamps, probably the same damn ones who killed those agents. Whatever is going on with you two needs to be tabled until we can figure this shit out, so knock it the fuck off before I get angry."

That had me hopping off the desk. "Is Ingrid okay?"

I asked about Ingrid and not Mags because, well, I wasn't Mags' biggest fan. Ingrid, though, would always and forever be on my good-guy list.

Thomas rubbed at his temple. "She's regrowing a pinkie finger but otherwise fine. They lost quite a few mid-level members of their nest, though. It was a blow. Luckily, they got backup. If they hadn't..." He shook his head as if the thought hurt him. "She should have called me earlier," he muttered under his breath. "I would have come."

I would have, too. Bounties and sleep be damned. "Do they need any help? Do we need to go?"

Anxiety prickled at my hands and feet—I wanted to be doing something. This X seemed to be in the middle of waging war, and it wasn't some piddly one-on-one shit. This was coordinated attacks. Strategic.

And I had no idea how to fight something like that.

"No," Thomas said, pinching his brow as if he was trying to stave off a headache. "We need to find out who killed Booth. Whoever did it, broke him out of prison, and was likely behind the ghoul attack. He was a loose end in need of snipping."

"Is this magic something we can track?" Dahlia piped up, the small witch practically hidden behind Bastian and Simon as they remained eyeing each other like rabid dogs. Grumbling, Dahlia snapped her fingers in front of Simon's nose, a spark from them zapping him right in the forehead.

"Ow," he grumbled, rubbing the red spot blooming

on his skin as he stumbled backward. "What did you do that for?"

Dahlia rolled her eyes. "Pay attention, dummy. Can we track the magic utilizing anything other than Sloane's poor nose? Employing her as our bloodhound isn't going to work and you know it."

Simon gave Dahlia a weighty glare as he continued to rub his forehead. Her eyes twitched a little and she moved to snap her fingers again. "Fine," he conceded, holding up his hands. "I could maybe do a locator working using Booth's blood. But that's a huge maybe."

Footsteps echoed throughout the short hallway to Gerry's office, and Emrys appeared at the door like an angry mama bear. "What's all this?"

"Strategy session and a reprieve from the smell," Simon answered quickly, his tone the picture of innocence.

It was solidly fake innocence, and Emrys wasn't fooled. "I thought I told you boys to table your bullshit. The circumstances haven't changed, you know."

"They're fine," Thomas said, sighing. "Just working out the kinks as we discuss how to locate Booth's killer. Nothing to worry about."

"And when exactly am I going to get my cemetery back?" Gerry asked, his gravelly voice practically echoing through the room. "It's bad enough I've got this one traipsing through here to bury her dead, but now I've got dismemberment to deal with? Ya'll need to keep your arcane shit to yourselves and leave us regular folk out of it."

I leaned to the side, around Bastian's bulk, to give Gerry the coldest of glares. "The first vamp I ever killed was a rapist and murderer, and his hunting ground was less than a block from here. Arcane shit has been in Whispering Pines a fuck of a lot longer than I have, so how about you keep your damn trap shut before I plant your tattling ass in your own damn cemetery?"

Gerry gave me an unbothered stare, like having my boss here was going to save him. Okay, it probably would, but he didn't need to know that. "I thought you only killed bad guys."

"That was before you ratted me out, Gerry. Had I known you were going to be a tattletale, I would have killed you and got my own damn backhoe. Dick."

Emrys sighed as if she was losing—or had already lost—her patience. "Enough, you two. Can we track the magic used or not?"

Simon waggled his hand. "I think so, but it's a huge maybe. If I were to venture a guess, Gerry interrupted whatever spell was being cast. The circle around Booth isn't complete, so technically, I could take a sample of his blood—what little of it he has left—and attempt a working to locate the caster. But..." He trailed off, like he was gearing up for something he really didn't want to say. "I think it might end up as a bust. There's something off about the spell work. It isn't just incomplete. It's backwards."

Grumbling, I skirted around the lot of them, the obvious answer hitting me square in the face.

I could read peoples' souls, right? I'd seen plenty in just a single swallow of Aunt Julie's blood, that I'd viscerally experienced her death. Although I in no way wanted to do that with Booth, maybe—and this was a bigger maybe than Simon's—I could take a taste of Booth's blood and track his killer that way. I'd done it hundreds of times before, hadn't I?

Granted, I did it when the perps were still alive, but...

*But what if it's just like Aunt Julie? What if you fall in and can never get out?*

That had my feet slowing their role and planting themselves in the manicured grass. The scent of Booth's death and the cloying magic hit me square in the face. Did I want that inside me? Did I want to be trapped in the agony of that death? I wasn't sure I could risk it.

"Please tell me you aren't doing what I think you are."

How did Bastian just manage to sneak up on me like that?

"I don't know. What do you think I'm doing?" I asked coyly, trying to stall for a better answer.

One of his arms came around my front, the heavy weight of it comforting as it rested on my collarbone. "I think," he whispered in my ear, "that you plan on reading him. It's too dangerous, Sloane. The last time you read from the dead…"

He didn't have to complete that sentence. I knew.

"I worry it will be worse for you with his. Who knows what atrocities he's committed? I don't know what you see when you read someone's blood, but I can't imagine that reading him will give you anything but nightmares."

Funnily enough, I didn't have nightmares too often, even with all I'd seen, all I'd read in the blood of deviants and murderers. The only thing I dreamt of was fire and blackness and screaming. And I had a feeling those things had nothing to do with what I gleaned from the blood of the damned souls I consumed.

"I'm not worried about nightmares," I answered, skipping over the rest of my misgivings.

He huffed in my ear as he pulled me closer. "But you are worried about everything else."

"What does Simon want to tell me?" I asked, changing the subject.

Bastian's grip got tighter before he let me go and sighed so heavily that it seemed to come from the tips of his toes. "Simon has a theory about why you are the way you are. It has merit, but it's completely bonkers. And I don't want to cause you undue harm if it turns out to be bullshit. So when I get a chance, I'll be researching the matter. Until then, I planned on making sure Simon kept his trap shut."

"It's bad, isn't it? The theory, I mean."

Bastian chuckled, shaking his head. "Honest?" he asked wincing, and I gave him a nod. "It's not great, but it's not the end of the world, either. It just is. I've been around a long time, and I've seen plenty of things that just are. But you haven't. All the things you've read in the blood of horrible people, you've only seen the worst of us. You've only seen the bad. You haven't seen all the good we are capable of. You haven't seen the wonder, the magic." He approached me again, wrapping me in his arms and pulling me to his chest. "You haven't seen enough to know that beauty and wonder are found even in the darkest of places."

I snorted, cuddling my head against his chest and squeezing him tight. "As beautiful as those words are, it's still a bunch of bullshit. You know that, right?"

Bastian pressed a kiss to the top of my head. "Yes, yes. I'm being an overprotective asshat. Give me a day to research Simon's claims before he drops a bomb on you? I'd hate for you to be forced to react to something that may not be true. You've gone through enough."

Squeezing him tighter, I turned my head to rest my chin between his pecs. Now that I could see his face, it struck me at just how worried he was. Bastian really didn't want to tell me whatever it was that had Simon in a twist. Meaning it had to be pretty bad. And if it was that bad, I probably didn't want to know unless I fucking well had to. "Fine. Twenty-four hours, and then you're spilling your guts. Deal?"

"Deal," he answered readily, like I was giving him a reprieve, and that gave me a healthy dose of pause.

Whatever Simon thought—whatever theory he had—it was probably true. And it was really, really bad.

Fabulous.

Reluctantly, I let Bastian go and took a step back, turning to head for what was left of Booth's body. A drop of his blood wasn't going to hurt, right? Granted, I'd never done a reading with a sample so small, but I could try, couldn't I?

"I thought—" Bastian began behind me, but he stopped himself.

Readily, I filled in the blanks. "You thought you'd talked me out of it?"

"Well, yeah," he answered, rushing to follow me. "Sloane, we don't know what will happen if you do this."

Scoffing, I halted my progress, swinging back to face him. "And we don't know what will happen if I don't. Booth knew X. He knew the man who killed my parents. He killed Aunt Julie. He was at the ghoul attack—he was at the prison break. He knew more information than I could possibly fathom. The last time I read his blood, I got nothing more than shadows. Now that he's dead, he can't fight me. Is this going to suck? Probably. But I can't just sit on my hands because you want the little lady to be safe, Bastian. Whatever it is? I'll heal."

I always did.

Rather than let him stop me, I turned and rushed toward Booth's remains, using whatever speed I had at my disposal. Then, everything seemed to slow down all at once. A flock of carrion birds burst into flight, my movements startling them from stalking their dinner. Their flapping wings moved at a snail's pace as they rose from the ground. Behind them a woman emerged from her crouch, the back of a monument no longer hiding her.

She seemed to be racing for me, her steps caught in

this sluggish pocket of time. Her hands waved, flapping just like those birds' wings as she screamed intelligible words.

I tried to stop—tried to duck—but as my foot made contact with the ground once more, the whole of the earth turned blindingly white as brilliant blistering pain blew me backward.

## 14

"I don't give a shit if you've been a medical doctor since Christ was a boy, Axel. You aren't taking her out of this room," Bastian growled. His voice had a fierce quality to it that spoke of violence and true death and a little bit of fear.

My eyes fluttered a bit, my lashes sticking together. It was so hard to open them, so I quit. My whole body felt as if it had gone through a meat grinder. I was in a bed, and I was inside, but other than that, I had no idea where I was.

"You're acting real big for your britches, son," Axel snarled. "All my equipment is down there—"

"Then bring it up here if you have to. Do you honestly think I'll let you treat her there while her aunt's body is still in your bloody freezer? If you can't treat her here, then I'll find someone else," Bastian hissed. "You aren't taking her away from me, do you understand?"

Weirdly, I wanted to tell Bastian thank you. As strange and possessive as his demands were, I didn't want to go to the med bay. I didn't want to be that close to Julie. Axel had always brought my blood to me—or Clem had. I hadn't been downstairs since...

"Leave it alone, Axel," Harper growled, her voice so close, it was as if I could reach out and touch her. Well, I could if I could convince my limbs to move. "You're fighting a losing battle in a war that has no purpose. Look. She's already healing. Just go get some blood," she instructed, her tone dismissive. "She'll need it."

Harper's words seemed to cause a chain reaction in my body. I craved blood—needed it in a way I couldn't describe. Everything hurt. Every single part of me felt as if it had been flash fried followed by an acid bath and then been tossed in a barbeque pit for good measure. But before I could say any of that, sounds dimmed, and the world fell away, and I was lost in the dark.

The next time I became aware of my surroundings, warm coppery heaven was dripping into my mouth. A few things became clear instantly, but I chose to ignore them in favor of swallowing the blissful nectar. First, I was naked in what seemed to be a bathtub, the freezing porcelain cooling my overheated skin.

*Burned, Sloane. You were burned.*

Well, at least my subconscious was paying attention because I sure as hell wasn't.

Second, someone held my mouth open, their gentle grip on my jaw making it so I could drink at all. Over the coppery scent of the blood, I recognized the person almost instantly. I'd know him anywhere. Bastian was feeding me, caring for me, and I needed to see if he was okay. The last thing I remembered was the white-hot heat of a blast, but he had been right behind me, hadn't he?

I opened my eyes by sheer force of will, the compulsion a base need that demanded to be satisfied. They put up a fight, but I muscled my lids open, quickly finding blazing green ones. As I continued to swallow the dregs of a blood bag, I cataloged his injuries—or at least the ones I could see. Bastian had a burn on his cheek, the baby pink of newly healed flesh stark against his tan. He had a stitched cut at his hairline, and his lip was split. Over the blood, I smelled smoke and ozone, and something else I couldn't identify. But all of that took a back seat to the stark worry ravaging his expression.

"You're awake," he murmured, relief easing the lines on his face.

Closing my mouth, I swallowed the last of the blood, and he pulled the bag away from my lips. Hunger clawed at my insides, and as much as I wanted to reassure him I was okay—that I'd be okay—I couldn't. I needed blood. Now.

And though it was not even a moment later, and another bag would be replacing the one I'd downed, I just couldn't wait. While I was all for him feeding me, I needed that blood. I needed it, or I was going to do something really, really stupid. And dangerous. I'd probably done enough stupid, dangerous things for the day.

A sound erupted from my throat as the hunger clawed at me, a keening sort of awful that hurt my own ears.

"It's okay," Bastian crooned. "I have more where that came from."

Before he could bring the bag to my lips, I snatched it away from him, sinking my fangs into the plastic and ripping. Tangy liquid flooded my mouth, and I gulped it down as fast as my throat would allow. All too quickly, it was gone, leaving me bereft before I caught sight of Bastian's pulse thrumming in his neck. He handed me another bag of blood, but it was ash on my tongue once I remembered what his tasted like.

Don't get me wrong, I still ripped into the fresh bag with the same fervor as I had the previous one, but I did it while also eyeing his neck. I didn't want this dead, human blood laced with bitter plastic. Oh, no. I wanted —no, craved—the potent, magic-laced ambrosia that flowed through his veins.

I needed it.

I could tell the exact moment Bastian realized he was out of bagged blood. His throat did this little bobbing thing as he swallowed, a faint trace of fear and lust spicing the air. He craved my bite, but he was scared, too.

*Me too, sweetheart. Me too.*

All the horrible things that could happen raced through my brain as my fingers found the lip of the tub, and I hauled myself out as he jumped to his feet.

"Sloane..."

I tilted my head so he knew I was listening, the ability to speak just out of my reach. Taking my first step out of the tub, he took one toward me, catching me in his arms when my knees threatened to give out. His spicy, delectable scent got stronger, lust winning out over the fear. That smelled better.

I didn't want him to be scared of me. I wanted him to want me.

That awful keening sound leaked out of my throat again as the hunger became too much for me to hold in. I didn't want him to fear me, but I most certainly wanted my lips at his neck, and his blood in my mouth, and his body surrounding me.

"Shh, sweetheart. Take what you need," he murmured, guiding me to his neck as he lifted me off my feet.

I couldn't say why his permission made the ache in my middle go away, or how I held off my hunger long enough for him to give it to me. All I knew was that I needed his blood, and now, I could have it. Quick as a whip, I struck, my fangs piercing his flesh at the exact moment my legs wound around his hips. Bastian's arms tightened, pressing my body further against his.

The first pull of his blood showed me all sorts of things. Our limbs tangled together as we moved in tandem, his lips on my skin, my flesh pebbling as a gasp erupted from my mouth, his fingers in my hair as we kissed and moved. I'd seen these images before. Nearly every time I'd taken his blood, I'd seen this scene play out almost as if it were a premonition. As if us being together this way was preordained, written in the stars.

My hands pawed at his shirt, the thin material no

match for my nails. I swallowed as I made quick work of the pesky fabric, ripping it from between us as if it were no more than tissue paper. My eyes practically rolled up in my head as the warmth of Bastian's flesh made contact with mine.

That single mouthful of his blood eased the ache in my bones, in my throat. It turned off the blistering agony of my healing burns, the flesh knitting itself back together. Everything felt better—everything felt new again. My brain cleared of pain as the heat of Bastian's skin continued to seep into me. It was the best heat. It was safety and lust and protection. Maybe something more—I hoped it was more.

His fingers found their way into my hair, a gentle tug reminding me not to take too much. Without any more prompting, I removed my fangs from his neck, licking the wounds so they would heal on their own. That earned me the best shudder, the vibration of it making everything inside me clench tight.

Without a word, Bastian's hand in my hair became insistent, guiding my face to his as he claimed my mouth in a kiss so hot, it made that damn fireball seem like a puff of smoke. It didn't seem to matter to him that I still had his blood on my tongue. It didn't matter that I was undoubtedly covered in the stuff. It didn't matter because nothing else did except him and me and the closest flat surface—horizontal or vertical, it really didn't matter which. Yanking on my hair, he broke our kiss before tasting the skin of my neck, biting my pulse point with his blunted teeth.

I couldn't stop the whimper that snaked up my throat or the way my hands roamed his skin, or how my hips did their best to grind against him. I wouldn't have stopped them even if I could have. His lips dipped lower as he hitched me higher on his hips, his mouth leaving a trail of biting kisses to my breast. The moan that came out of my mouth once his lips closed around my nipple was loud enough to wake the dead.

And then he moved, one arm releasing me to snap his fingers as his feet made tracks to wherever he needed to take us. I hoped he was going somewhere with a bed.

A big one.

"I need you," I gasped, my hands finding his face before pressing my lips to his again. My back met cool sheets, the coldness of them a stark contrast from the blisteringly luscious heat of Bastian's skin against mine. He settled between my legs, his hand cupping the back of my head as his fingers wound themselves into my hair.

"That's good, love, because I fucking well need you, too." Bastian's words hit me with the sweetest of blows. "I need you today, and I'll need you tomorrow, and on and on until the sun quits burning. I'm yours, you understand?" His green eyes flashed as the seriousness of what he was telling me fell on me like a warm blanket.

Tears stung my eyes before the question I didn't want to ask fell from my mouth. "Promise?"

He nodded, brushing his nose against mine before following suit with his lips. "I promise."

I couldn't help it—not that I thought I'd ever want to help it—I kissed him with every good thing I had left in me. My hands roamed over his skin, letting his heat, his life, his vitality bleed into me. Just like his blood in my mouth, every bit of his energy fueled me. Every single brush of his mouth and caress of his fingers brought me back to life. His mouth moved from mine as he kissed and licked every bit of skin he could reach, his fingers finding my center as his mouth swiftly followed suit. His lips and tongue devoured me as his hot hands clutched me to him, refusing to let me wriggle away.

The man feasted on me, taking everything I had as he wrenched moan after moan out of me. The slide of his tongue, the gentle nibbles of my flesh, sent me into the most delicious frenzy. It was almost too much, too big. What I was feeling couldn't possibly be an orgasm. This was a tsunami and an earthquake and a hurricane all at once. This was... He twisted his fingers inside me, and the dam broke. A flash fire of pleasure erupted over my flesh, and I practically screamed.

Wanting him seemed to be all I could think of—it was in every breath, every kiss, every touch. I wanted him inside me as my fangs pierced his neck. I wanted him invading every part of me. I wasn't sure if I said that out loud or if Bastian could read my mind, but before I could take my next breath, Bastian was kissing me as he rolled us, the taste of my arousal on his tongue making me crave him more.

He sat us up as I reached for his pants. But instead of denim, all I found was him.

*God bless mages and magic and whatever sorcery got him naked for me.*

My fingers wrapped around his length as a groan rolled up his throat and into my mouth. I'd had the mother of all orgasms, and already I needed him to give me another one. Rising up on my knees, I slicked him through my wetness, not taking him inside. I couldn't say why I wanted to torture him this way, until his eyes flashed that brilliant bright green again.

His growl tore through the room as his fingers found my hair, tightening just enough to make me crazy.

"Give yourself what you need," he whispered against my mouth. "Give me what I need."

And so, I did. Notching his length against my center,

I lowered myself onto him, the unbelievably sexy moan that fell from his lips only compounding the bliss of him filling me. I almost couldn't move, the fear I wouldn't be able to take that much goodness, that much pleasure freezing me—right up until his arms banded around my back, his fingers making a home in my hair. Then he nibbled on my bottom lip as he gently thrust upward. My hips moved to answer his, following the rhythm he set. Each retreat was agony, and each return was paradise, the punishing pace killing me and saving me at the same time.

But I didn't bite him yet.

So distracted by every sensation, I nearly forgot about taking his blood. Then he broke our kiss, and all I could smell was our desire. All I could feel was him. All I could see was his face. All I could hear were the noises we made as our bodies glided together and the beat of his heart. My fangs practically ached as the thrum of his pulse rang in my ears.

"Take what you need," Bastian growled, his voice thick and full of gravel.

Without a thought, I struck, piercing the tender skin of his neck with my aching fangs. The bliss of his blood, the feel of him inside me, the groan erupting from his throat. God, it was all too much, too good. Whatever hold I had on my sanity left me then—left us both—our releases crashing over us in wave after wave of molten pleasure.

I couldn't remember how long we stayed connected, or how many times we came together afterward. It could have been moments or days.

All I knew—deep down in that cold, shriveled thing I called a heart—was that I was in love with Sebastian Cartwright, and if anyone hurt him, they would have hell to pay.

## 15

I woke up before Bastian did, and like the smart girl I tried to be, I stayed put, studying his sleeping face. Asleep, all the worry melted from his expression. The deep groove between his eyebrows eased, the near-permanent clench to his jaw gone. We'd slept facing each other, my head pillowed on his arm, our legs tangled together along with the bedsheets.

The desire to stay right here in this little bubble of happy filled me. I didn't want to move, or speak, or ask questions. Bastian and I would live here in this room forever and the world wouldn't touch us, and all the bad things would let us be. It was an irrational thought quickly dashed by reality.

"I can feel you thinking," he grumbled, his eyes still shut. His arms closed around me, and I had no choice but to be swept up in them. "No thoughts. Just content, blissed-out afterglow. I must insist on it."

Pressing my nose into the center of his chest, I breathed him in, the crisp hairs tickling my face. "That sounds nice."

I clutched him to me, settling in to never move again, when a god-awful pounding rattled the bedroom door.

"Go away," he called, his arms tightening just a smidge too tight.

"Sebastian August Cartwright," Simon yelled through the door, "you get your ass out of that room this instant. It's bad enough I had to pick the sound warding, but did you really have to use the Faustian defense? You caught my favorite shirt on fire, you ass."

I put a hand on his chest, pushing away so I could look him in the eye. "You set your brother on fire?"

Bastian rolled his eyes. "Only a little, and it's his fault for picking my locks. He could have just as easily sent me a message, but he decided to get cute. I take zero responsibility for his poor planning."

Simon pounded on the door again. "Emrys is insisting that we come to dinner, so put on some clothes and get down there before she decides to test your magic against hers."

At the thought of solid food, my stomach rumbled something fierce, the hungry gurgle probably loud enough to be heard downstairs. I was more than satisfied on the blood front. Bastian's magic-laced offerings had likely powered me up until the end of time. I worried that I might have taken too much from him.

But his skin appeared no worse for wear, and his eyes still had that twinkle of mischief and desire and... Bastian gently clutched my wrist as he reeled me in for a kiss, and for some reason, I didn't care about the possibility of our bubble being popped. I didn't care about anything at all.

A louder bang rattled the door before Thomas' voice echoed through the wood. "Don't make me drag you two out."

I broke the kiss, somehow finding myself straddling Bastian. "Party pooper. We'll be there in a minute."

"Do we have to?" Bastian whined, nuzzling his face between my breasts as he cupped my ass in his hands, which naturally made everything inside me clench.

Did we have to go? I mean, really? Couldn't we—

My stomach took that opportunity to release the mother of all growls.

"Fine, fine," he muttered, sighing. "I must keep my lady fed." He moved his hands to my hips before lifting me up and setting me on the floor. Then he yanked a robe from the back of his bathroom door, holding it out for me, and I slipped into it. Before I knew it, he was in front of me again, tying the belt. "If I shower with you in here, we'll never leave. Meet you downstairs in ten?"

*Can I wash all the blood and sex off me in ten minutes?* Looking at the hope and happiness on this face? I was damn sure going to try.

"Deal."

After taking the fastest shower on record and donning jeans and a black T-shirt—one aptly emblazoned with the phrase, "Please don't make me kill you"—I raced down the stairs, my booted feet clomping as I went. Hair still wet and piled on my head, I realized about ten seconds too late that I wasn't wearing any jewelry, as the whole of the dining room came to an abrupt hush. I swear there were practically crickets chirping and everything.

"Dear sweet baby Jesus in a manger, what in the ever-loving fuck sticks is going on with your face?" Clem exclaimed, her thick Southern drawl softening the blow just a tad.

I hadn't bothered to look in a mirror—I hadn't had the time—so I didn't know if I resembled a burn victim, or if it was just the regular old *Skelator* that was getting Clem's goat. My gaze found Thomas' instantly. "My necklace burned off, didn't it?"

"Oh, most definitely," he answered, a smile creeping across his lips. "As did most of your flesh, your hair, and a few fingers. As you can tell, it all grew back, and in less than twenty-four hours, too. I know ancients who can't do that. Myself included."

Wincing, I tried to think of a good explanation, but I didn't know any more than they did.

"Well, Clem..." I began, ready to spill the beans—not that I knew exactly what those beans were when the faint trill of someone approaching made me smile.

"I think she's beautiful just like she is," Bastian said from behind me, dropping a kiss to the side of my neck. "There's no reason to wear a glamour at home. You don't wear yours."

He tagged my hand, pulling me behind him to the two available seats. He pulled out my chair before taking his own, and all the while, everyone goggled at us like we were Martians. Okay, I totally couldn't blame them. A couple of months ago, Bastian and I were at each other's throats—literally.

"Point taken, and I agree," Clem replied, setting down a covered platter on the table. "I don't think Sloane needs to wear a glamour at home. I just want to know why she's flickering like a Halloween decoration at the dinner table."

I was glad I wasn't drinking anything because I would have covered Dahlia in it when I busted out laughing.

"A Halloween decoration. Oh, man, that's good." I wiped at the mirthful tears. It was a much better way to think about it. I was a spooky décor piece rather than a monster. I'd totally take it.

"Look who's talking," Harper accused, reaching for the basket of rolls. "You could pass for Bride of Frankenstein's sassy younger sister."

Clem snorted. "Touché, and thank you. That's the nicest compliment anyone's ever given me."

"I aim to please," Harper volleyed back around a mouthful of roll.

Simon tapped his fingers on the table, his impatience ready to erupt from his ears. "So, no one is going to mention the witch in the dungeon, or the fact that Sloane obviously has something wrong with her, or the fact that—"

"Whoa, whoa, whoa." I held up a hand, stopping his tirade. "Can I not get some food in my belly before you start in on everything? I need sustenance to deal with whatever the hell happened to me, the aforementioned witch in the dungeon—glad that's getting some use, by the way—and the veritable mountain of other shit going on. Slow your roll."

Simon glared in my direction, not happy at all that I'd cut him off.

"Exactly. I know you've been dying to discuss this

particular quagmire, Simon, but Sloane is right," Emrys scolded, loading her plate with fried chicken and greens. "Can't we have one nice meal with each other before the world falls in?"

He huffed in his chair, crossing his arms like a petulant child.

"What I wanna know is, how in the hell did you keep Simon out of your room so long?" Axel asked, a chuckle laced in his question as he loaded mashed potatoes on his plate. "That boy has been trying to bust in there for hours."

Bastian snorted, passing me a platter of grilled cod. "Faustian defense. Prevents a blood tie from breaking a ward. I knew no one else but my brother would interrupt." He shook his head. "Honestly, after six hundred years, one would think you'd know better."

Shock flooded my limbs as I froze mid-pass to Thomas. I goggled at Bastian for a moment or twelve. "You dirty old man, you. Dating a woman so young. *Tsk, tsk, tsk.*"

I was joking... mostly.

He leaned my way, eyeing my face with amusement. "You've killed more people in a year than I have in six hundred. I figure that makes us about even. Don't you?"

I couldn't fault that logic. The certainty that I was

stupidly in love with the man meant that breaking up with him was pretty much off the table. "I'll allow it."

"Dear god, are they always going to be like this?" Harper griped.

"I'm sure I'll piss her off eventually," Bastian answered, his gaze never leaving my face as he leaned back.

"You know this means I'll have to separate you two on jobs," Emrys said through a sigh.

"Oh, no, you won't." Of all the people I expected to say that, Dahlia wasn't the one. Still, she pointed her fork at our fearless leader as if she was ready to stab her with it. "I want my partner back. No offense to Bastian, but he steals all the magical thunder on every single job. What is the point of having two magic-users on the same team? Not just no, but hell no. Let those two have each other, and give me back Thomas, or so help me, I'll—"

"Fine, fine." Emrys held up her hands in surrender. "You can be paired with Thomas. But if they mess up and let high-value targets get away to save each other or some other nonsense, I'll have to reevaluate."

Dahlia pivoted in her chair and pointed her fork at us. "Don't you dare mess this up, you hear me?"

Wide-eyed, all I could do was nod.

"Aww, Dahlia," Thomas said, batting his eyelashes at her. "I didn't know you cared."

She snorted in answer. "Oh, shut up."

After loading my plate with more food than I thought I could possibly eat, I dug in, the inane chatter of friends and family surrounding me. It hit differently than the first night I'd sat in this same chair. It used to grate on me, the feeling of not belonging. I still thought *I* was a freak, sure, but I was wanted here in this family of freaks.

When I had a full belly, and the rest of the table were picking at the dregs of the food, I wiped my face with the napkin before sitting forward in my chair. Simon— who had been nearly silent the whole meal—focused on me.

"Okay. My belly is full, and I'm happy and content for the first time in a year. Let me enjoy it for five more minutes, and then you can introduce me to the witch in the dungeon who tried to blow me up."

"Sloane," Bastian murmured, the plea in his tone a testament to the level of bad coming my way.

"Twenty-four hours was the deal. I figure that's been up for a while now."

"As you wish."

But I didn't wish. Not at all.

## 16

The dungeon was just as I remembered it—not that I expected much to change in the two months since I'd been here last. Several empty cells encased in rune-covered bars and cinderblock dotted one side of the Night Watch's de facto dungeon.

Bastian had given me a run-down of what happened in the time I'd been lost to my injuries. Evidently, what Simon thought about the circle surrounding Booth's body had only been partially accurate. It had been a backward working, an incomplete circle. However, what he'd thought was a safe space was actually a spell within a spell.

One to kill.

One to neutralize.

And the wrong one was incomplete.

To my astonishment, the witch was not in my old cell. When I'd been brought here a couple of months ago, my cell was furnished with a bed, a toilet, a desk, and a screen for privacy. Evidently, Emrys had thought it would take some convincing to get me to join their ragtag bunch of misfits. Either that, or they'd wanted me comfortable before I was served up to the person who posted my bounty.

But the witch did not reside in my former home. No, they'd placed her in one of the barren cells with a bucket for a toilet and not much else. The runes surrounding the cell were blazing orange, even though no one was near them. What little I knew about those runes could fill a thimble, but I figured they were glowing because this witch was simply made of magic. They were making her uncomfortable to keep her contained.

At our approaching footsteps, the witch looked up. Mahogany hair fell in messy waves down her back, her face and clothes streaked in soot and blood, an unhealing burn marring her jaw. Hazel eyes flashed for a moment before she winced, the burn of the runes blazing hotter.

Gingerly, she stood, favoring her right leg over her left. "It's good to see you again, Sloane. I was worried about you."

The way she said my name—as if she knew me, as if we'd spoken a hundred times before—grated on my nerves.

"Do I know you?" I asked, settling onto a folding metal chair as Simon and Bastian acted as my sentries. Even Thomas had accompanied us for good measure.

The witch winced, wilting back down to the floor. "I appeared quite a bit different when you knew me. My name is Celeste Warner, but you knew me as Mrs. Ida Blumenthal, the sweet old lady down the street. Sorry for the deception. It was…" She paused, thinking on the right word before settling on, "necessary."

*Mrs. Blumenthal? The same lady that helped me with my bloody knees when Otis dragged me down the street?*

"Was trying to kill me necessary or just a happy accident?" I remembered her rushing me right before I activated the circle and blew myself to kingdom come. I nearly shuddered at the memory of the pain but managed to hold it in.

Celeste shook her head. "Had I been allowed to finish my circle, none of that would have happened. And in case you don't recall, I was trying to get you to stop. It's not my fault your boyfriend dicked around with time magic." Her gaze shifted from me to spear Bastian with a glare. "You should know better."

Bastian huffed, his cheeks reddening. "Says the

woman who used outlawed grave magic to murder a man."

*So that's the scent tickling my nose.* Funny. It didn't seem too horrible now that Booth's corpse wasn't right next to me.

"Like you wouldn't have done the same," she retorted, giving Bastian a scathing glower. "And Booth McCall deserved to die. With the spell imbued in his flesh, we got lucky. Dollars to donuts he was coming here, ready to kill you all for hiding her. Don't act like that wasn't the end goal." The witch massaged at her temples, as if just talking to us was giving her a headache. "You know, I didn't even want to be there. Had your mother listened to me, I wouldn't have been." She chuckled as she continued to massage her head. "Twenty years in the same house, wearing the same glamour, watching out for you, and it was for nothing. X still found you. He still keeps finding you." Tears gathered in her eyes as she sniffed.

I stood, staring down at the witch as rage prickled my skin. "What do you know about X?"

The laugh that erupted from her mouth was bitter. "I know that he came after you just like he came for my daughter. My Aurora was beautiful. Sweet. Innocent. Never hurt a soul in her short, short life. I did everything I could to keep her hidden. Given who her father was, all the unrest his children were causing, I didn't want her caught up in it. But I couldn't hide her from him." Her lips trembled, her voice growing thick as she continued, "I came home to our house on fire, and Rory..." She shook her head. "I swore I would keep an eye on you. That you wouldn't have the same fate as my girl. I swore to him that I would."

"Swore to who?" I probed. "What are you talking about?"

Frowning, Celeste swiped at her tears, examining me as if she'd never seen me before in her life. "Wow. Your mother really kept you in the dark, didn't she? I swore to your *father*. Azrael."

Bastian and Simon shifted, but I moved even closer to the bars.

"My father was Peter Cabot," I insisted, the hissed declaration coming from clenched teeth. "I don't know what you're playing at, but you've got me mixed up with someone else."

Celeste searched the ceiling for something, maybe patience. "Why do I feel as if I'm on an episode of *Maury*?" Sighing, she brought her chin down, staring me dead in the eye. "Peter Cabot raised you, but he did not provide the genetic material that made you what you are. Just like my daughter, your father is Azrael, the Angel of Death."

"Bullshit."

Celeste's laugh was mirthless. "You'd like to think so, wouldn't you? That everything you knew was real. That you weren't lied to every single moment of your life? I get that. Had your mother listened to me, had she hidden you better, I bet you'd still be in the dark. Still thinking you were human. That she was."

I didn't want to hear this woman lie to me. "Fuck you, lady. Fuck. You." Rage nearly propelled me against the bars, the burn of the runes less important than telling this woman off. "You don't know the first thing about my mother. You don't know the first thing about me."

Celeste struggled to her feet, getting closer to the bars, too. "I know you died that night."

Her words hit me like a fist to the gut, faint images of my mother pressing on my chest filtering through my brain.

"What?" I breathed, but Celeste was on a roll.

"After X slit your father's throat, he came after you, and because she'd bound your powers, because she'd told you nothing of what you were, you were no match for him. Funnily enough, he was probably going to leave your mother alive—just like me and Rory. Leave her to her grief and loss. Leave her alone in the world. But your mother tried to bring you back as a vampire, and it didn't work. She died trying to bring you back, trying to fix her mistake." Celeste shook her head, a bitter sort of pity on her face. "He killed her just like Peter. I know that *I* got you out. I know that *I* took you to your father. I know you're not alive and not undead. I know *lots* of things, Sloane."

The world was spinning, but I seemed to be staying still.

More and more flashes filled my brain.

My father lying in a pool of blood.

A man in a suit with a giant knife.

Purple magic...

Staggering back, I shook my head. "No."

I whispered that word—denying her and her awful statements, but I knew they were true. I knew. My whole body shook with the reality of what she was saying. "Tell me the rest."

"I took you to Azrael, ready to die because I'd failed you. Because I didn't get there in time. Because I didn't stop that bastard from taking you like he took Rory. But Azrael didn't want to let you go—didn't want another one of his children to be lost."

My back met the cinderblock wall as the runes around us glowed brighter, hotter.

"What did he do to me?" The question came out as an accusation, which it most certainly was.

Celeste's expression was a ravaged sort of agony that told me all sorts of things I didn't want to know. *This* was what Simon had figured out. *This* was the truth I didn't want to know. And man, was it going to hurt.

"Azrael did something he couldn't have done for any of his other children. By the time I got you to him, you'd been gone maybe a day, but your mother had attempted to transition you to a vampire. He couldn't make you alive again—you'd been dead too long—but he could imbue you with a piece of himself. He could bring you back by making you like him. You had a fraction of his powers already—they were just bound. So he weakened himself, giving you more so you would come back, so you could live in this realm."

I shook my head, my breaths coming in hurried pants.

"You aren't alive. And you aren't undead. Ask yourself, Sloane, what else is there?"

*My mother was screaming, pressing on my chest over and over again. Her hands were hard, weighty as if they were fifty-pound dumbbells just chilling on my ribcage. I wanted to answer her, but I just couldn't. Everything hurt. Everything. From my toes, all the way up to my hair, every single bit of me felt as if I was being flash fried by a blowtorch, followed by an acid bath.*

*This was death.*

*I couldn't understand her words, either. I was either going deaf, or she was speaking gibberish, and I was in so much pain it really didn't matter. It didn't matter when the agony made me want to die—made me hope relief was coming.*

*The room around us was hazy at best. Smoke swirled and bloomed in a halo around her head as an odd purple light whirled up her arms. And she was crying. Or at least I thought she was. A tiny trail of a tear dropped from her eye and hit me on the cheek. I wanted to wipe it away. Wanted to tell her I was okay, but I couldn't do that, either.*

*Her strong fingers gripped my shoulders, and she pulled me into her arms, hugging me to her chest as if she was saying goodbye.*

*That's when I saw the flames.*

*That's when I saw my dad lying in a pool of his own blood in the middle of the living room.*

*That's when I saw the man in the gray suit, his face shrouded within the shadows, kneeling over my father.*

*He held a wicked-looking knife in his hand—bigger than a dagger but smaller than a sword—the awful blade coated in my father's blood. He rose from his crouch, an awful laugh bubbling up his throat as the sound danced over the roar of the flames and my mother's sobs.*

*And he was coming for us.*

*No, he was coming for her. Pale fingers found her hair, yanking her backward as the sword raked against her throat.*

*Blood poured from her neck as her grip loosened, and I fell backward.*

*The man examined me, hovering over my rapidly dying body, a gleeful smile on his face as his violet gaze bore into me.*

*"Give Azrael my best, won't you?" he said before plunging the dagger into my chest.*

My legs gave out as I slid to the ground, the rough cinderblock pulling at my shirt. Ragged breaths sawed in and out of my lungs as the runes burned bright around us, their heat searing into my skin.

*You aren't alive. And you aren't undead. Ask yourself, Sloane, what else is there?*

The answer was so simple and so complicated at the same time. I wasn't alive and I wasn't undead.

I was just dead.

## 17

"**I** have to keep my mouth shut for days, but you just let some stranger toss a brick at her head and hope for the best?" Simon shouted, getting in Bastian's personal space.

*Is this man seriously upset he didn't get the chance to ruin my entire worldview and the memory of my parents? Because that's just wrong—on a bevy of fucking levels.*

Bastian practically growled. "Just because you're the resident death mage doesn't mean it's your responsibility, nor is it even appropriate for you to tell her. And had I known this lady had all the answers, I—"

Simon snarled, cutting his brother off. "You would have done fuck all. You're just glad it wasn't one of us who did the dirty work."

I hated the thought as soon as it entered my head, but Simon wasn't wrong. I was sort of glad Celeste was the one to tell me, and not someone I actually gave a shit about.

"Knock it off, children," Thomas rumbled, his voice a hell of a lot closer than I thought it'd be. His shoulder bumped mine as he settled on the ground. "You can duke it out later when we're not in the middle of a crisis."

I let out a small chuckle, the idea of Thomas calling six-hundred-year-old Bastian a child completely preposterous to me. That and the thought that we would ever *not* be in a crisis. "Oh, out with it, Simon," I insisted. "Anything else you want to add? Am I really a swamp thing that needs to be taken out back and shot or something?"

Really, it wouldn't surprise me at this point. According to Celeste, my father was the Angel of Death. *Because that was a thing.*

"Not that I know of. She had more information than I did. I just had a theory based on Isis, your flickering face, and that story Thomas told me about you trying to die. You kept trying, but you couldn't..." Simon shook his head as he rubbed a hand over his mouth. "I had an errant thought that took root. You'd tried killing yourself and it never worked because you were already dead."

"So, I was a suicidal dead girl," I said, laughing. "The irony there is just beautiful." I puckered my lips and did a little chef's kiss.

Celeste snorted. "No wonder you look like that. How many times have you 'died' in the last year?" She used air quotes and everything, the bitch.

"I have no idea," I replied, picking myself up off the cold stone floor. "It's not like I kept a running tally. I was a little preoccupied with killing bad guys and stopping people from getting murdered on the streets. Excuse the fuck out of me."

She gave me an exasperated stare that could undoubtedly peel the paint off a car. "You're essentially chipping away at yourself every time you do that, stupid."

"Yes, and I totally know exactly what you mean by that. Don't elaborate at all. I'm sure I'll figure it out." One thing I could say about myself: my sarcasm was on point.

Celeste rolled her eyes so hard I was surprised they didn't roll on out of her head. "Think about it for about a nanosecond. You are the composition of a death deity and a blood mage, only now you have far more death deity essence in you. Every time you 'die,' you're chipping away at the blood mage part of yourself that makes you... well... *you* because the death deity shit can't die. *Duh.* No wonder you look like a walking embodiment of death. You keep fucking around and you will be."

My eyes popped wide as the reality of my situation hit me. Then the nausea landed squarely on my tongue, and I raced out of the dungeon to find the closest receptacle. The downstairs powder room bore the brunt of my reaction, the last truth bomb just a bit too much for me to handle. Heaving in the toilet, I begged my stomach to quit volleying up my dinner. Cool hands found my overheated skin, a wet washcloth on the back of my neck easing some of the worst of it.

"You're going to be all right, love. Just breathe." Bastian's sweet words filtered in my ears, as wetness gathered in my eyes.

*How can he want me? I am... I'm a monster.*

The tears came in earnest then, the heavy weight of despair practically suffocating me. With my heaves over, he gathered me in his arms, cradling me there as he got comfortable on the ground. "Shh, love. It's okay. You're going to be okay."

"No, it's not," I sobbed, as the truth of it all came crashing over me.

X had already killed everyone I'd ever loved once before. He'd taken everything from me—even my life. He'd tried to kill me over and over again, hurting anyone who'd gotten in his way.

"I don't understand. Why does he want me dead? I've never done anything to him. I've never—" I stopped abruptly and shook my head, the tears falling faster than I could wipe them away. "Why did he rip everything I've ever known away from me? He..." I had to swallow the lump in my throat as the memory of my father, dead, on the floor in a pool of his own blood, flashed in my mind, quickly followed by X slashing my mother's throat.

Shuddering, I tried to wipe the newfound knowledge from my brain.

"He killed them right in front of me, and then he stabbed me." An echo of the agony of his blade piercing my heart radiated from my chest, and I rubbed at the spot. "I think I was already mostly dead by that point, but he needed to make sure."

*And he laughed while he did it.*

I didn't tell him the worst part of it all. The part I didn't want to think about and would have me avoiding mirrors for the rest of my life—however long that would be.

This X? He looked like me—or like I did now. White-haired, purple eyes, pale skin, high cheekbones.

All too soon I connected the dots.

He'd killed Celeste's daughter, just as he'd killed me. And he used a blood curse to do it when his efforts hadn't panned out like he wanted.

X wasn't *just* family.

He wasn't just *my* blood.

X was my brother.

Scrambling out of Bastian's lap, I staggered downstairs. Celeste had answers and she was going to cough them up one way or another.

Simon and Thomas were hissing in a corner, their discussion less important than the question I needed to ask Celeste.

"How do I contact Azrael?" The inquiry burst from my lips like a shotgun blast. "You talked to him, right? How do I do it?"

Celeste stared at me as if I'd grown another head. "You want to *talk* to a death deity?"

Did I want to just talk to the man? Absolutely not. I wanted to punch him in the face for taking my choices away from me. I wanted to set his dumb ass on fire. I wanted...

"Yes," I replied, my feigned calm fooling no one. "I want to talk to the man you call my father. I want to hear it *from him* how I came to be what I am. He has answers that I don't."

Totally rational answer. Too bad that was only the half of what I wanted to ask. I'd also appreciate knowing who in the blue fuck gave him the right to make me like this. I was super interested in that answer.

"I don't know if that's a good idea, Sloane," Thomas murmured, his and Simon's conversation dying off at my impromptu interrogation. "Azrael isn't at your beck and call."

I snorted derisively, craning my neck to look Thomas in the eye. "I am one hundred percent positive that I didn't fucking ask you. But just in case I did, wouldn't you want to ask the man who turned you into a monster against your will a question or two?"

Thomas' eyes popped wide in surprise, and he took a step back. "Point made."

"Exactly." Shifting my attention back to our prisoner, I repeated my query. "How do I contact Azrael?" She opened her mouth to respond, but I held up a hand to stop her. "Before you start on some bullshit, please keep in mind that I have reached the *very* end of my rope, I do *not* consider you an ally, and I'm *incredibly* good at getting the answers I seek one way or another. So, you can decide how I get my answers, but please note, that I *am* getting them. Either by you telling me or showing me through your blood—and I *really* don't give a fuck which."

A faint thread of alarm crossed Celeste's face, and she backed up a step. "You're not going to hurt him, right?"

All I could do was laugh. Did she honestly believe I'd be able to hurt Death himself? "I haven't decided, but don't worry your pretty little head about it. If I can't manage to kill myself, I'm thinking I'll have a hell of a time trying to kill him."

She pursed her lips at me as if that rationalization rubbed her the wrong way. "Fine. If you want to pitch a fit like a toddler to your daddy, be my guest." She massaged at her temples as she gave me an exasperated huff. "Find an unwarded spot on the property and call for him with your mind. Azrael is in tune with his children. He'll hear you and come if he can. I don't make any promises that he'll actually come when you call, but summoning him requires a sacrifice I doubt you'd be willing to make."

I frowned at her until it dawned on me. By sacrifice, she meant a real one.

A life.

Yeah, I'd definitely be trying door number one.

"Thank you," I chirped, the picture of politeness, as if I hadn't just threatened to bleed her dry before pivoting on my heel to exit the dungeon. I probably would have been able to follow through with my intended course of action—which was to scream at the sky until Azrael himself showed his stupid face—if I weren't staring down two mages and a vampire.

"What now?" I complained, and if I happened to sound like a whiney brat, well, then so be it.

"Do you really think summoning a death deity is a good idea?" Simon asked, echoing Thomas' earlier question.

"Considering I won't have to kill anyone to do it, yeah, I do." I crossed my arms over my chest as I glared at the death mage. Yeah, he more than likely knew way more than I did on the subject, but I seriously doubted he had put it all together.

"X killed my parents right in front of me before he stabbed me in the chest." I ticked that point off on my thumb. "Then, when that didn't work, he used the Night Watch to find me, putting a three-million-dollar bounty on my head." I raised my index finger. "When that didn't pan out, he got Booth to kidnap you, sending an army of ghouls to do his bidding." Middle finger. "And when that didn't work, he doubled down with a blood curse." My ring finger went up. "Now we have a prison break, a sacked ABI building, and whatever bullshit spell Booth was filled with." All five fingers were up now. "How much fucking collateral damage has his quest to murder me caused? Think about it. I'll wait."

Recrossing my arms over my chest, I waited a full thirty seconds in stone-cold silence.

"Oh, you don't have a retort to that? *Shocker.* But let me break it down further for you. Every single person in this house is in danger because of me. You, your brother, Thomas, Emrys, Dahlia, Harper, Axel, Clem, and even Isis. All of you. Because this is where I lay my head. This is where I found shelter. This is where I found love and acceptance and friends. If you honestly believe that I wouldn't use every single weapon I had at my disposal to protect you, you're fucking dreaming. So yeah, I'm summoning a death deity. You got a problem with that?"

"Anyone ever tell you that you're fucking frightening when you're mad?" Celeste asked, and I whipped my head to glare at her.

"Not twice," I replied before turning back to the men in my way. "Move."

Thomas and Simon did as they were told, but Bastian stayed right where he was. "If you're going to go do something stupid, I'm not letting you go alone."

I pointed my index finger right at his face like I'd seen my mother do a hundred times to my dad. "No funny business. Got it?"

Bastian gave me the Boy Scout salute, as if the man had ever been a Boy Scout a day in his life.

"I promise, 'no funny business,' as you call it. I just want to watch your back." A slight smile curled his lips. "Plus, you don't know where the wards are."

He had me there.

## 18

The warmth of Bastian's fingers laced with mine helped distract me from the reality of what I was about to do. A few minutes ago, I had plenty of bravado, but as we walked through the high grasses on the edge of the ward, all my earlier confidence seemed to be on sabbatical.

"You don't have to do this, you know," Bastian murmured, gently squeezing my hand in his. "Celeste may know more. We could question her. Maybe—"

"If she had more info, she would have told us. Don't get me wrong, she probably has a ton of answers, just not to the questions I need to ask. She has no more of a way to stop X than we do."

*She doesn't know why he made me this way either, don't forget that one.*

Bastian seemed to think about that for a moment. "True, but she does have more questions to answer. Like how did you end up on your grave? Why were you just left there with nothing? No answers, no home, no idea what you were or what happened. Who does that?"

Yeah, that was on my list for dear old dad. Just after why his son was trying to kill me, and how I could attempt to kill him first.

Bastian pulled me to a stop when I ignored his griping. "You amaze me, you know? When your case came across our radar, I thought you were just another Rogue. Another monster to be put down. How you survived this last year after what you went through..." He released my hand to cup my face. "You're a goddamn miracle, Sloane."

Funny, I didn't feel like one. But with Bastian's hands on my face, with his beautiful bottle-green eyes staring at me as if I was a treasure? Yeah, I could believe it for a little while.

"You're just saying that because you want back in my pants. Don't lie."

He stepped fully into my space, his front brushing mine as he let my face go to latch onto my hips. "Oh, I definitely want back in your pants, but I mean this, too. You're a fucking miracle."

He lowered his head, gently sweeping his lips against mine, deepening the kiss as soon as I parted my lips. His tongue caressed mine, and I was lost to his safety, to his warmth, to him.

"I was under the impression you needed to talk to me," a deep voice called, shocking the shit out of both of us.

One second, we were kissing, and the next, Bastian had me behind him, a ball of fire in his hand. Well, until the fire in his palm winked out at the same time I heard a snap.

"Was I mistaken?" the voice asked.

*How stupid are we? I don't even have a weapon on me—not that I need one, but still.*

Peering around Bastian's bulk, I spied a tall dark-haired man in a black suit. His black hair spilled down to his shoulders, and a long scar marred what I thought was a decently handsome face.

But unlike X, I didn't resemble this man at all.

"Ah, yes." He paused, gesturing to his suit. "This is a comforting depiction of Death for most humans. They expect me to be a dark-suited thing carrying a scythe. I suppose I could go for broke with the hood, but they're dreadfully hot."

A wash of cold dread filled me at his response.

Mostly because I hadn't asked him an actual question. Not out loud, anyway. "I didn't say anything."

He shrugged. "Doesn't mean I didn't hear you. You read information in blood—I read thoughts. We each have our own talents."

I touched Bastian's back, trying to comfort him, but he seemed frozen or encased in stone. Bastian stared ahead, unblinking.

"What did you do to him?" I asked, fully stepping out from behind him and moving in front to protect him with my body.

"Nothing. When we're done talking, he'll wake right back up. I simply prefer to discuss your grievances alone."

Grievances. As if my questions were a nuisance. *Asshole.*

"I heard that," he muttered, frowning at me like I was a naughty child.

I narrowed my eyes, crossing my arms. "I meant you to. You turned me into a monster after your son took everything I ever loved away from me. *Grievances.* Death deity or not, you can kiss my ass."

Azrael took a deep breath, likely searching the cosmos for patience. But I had questions, and I was going to ask them.

"Why don't we look alike? I resemble X, why don't I look like you?"

Azrael sighed and snapped his fingers. Instantly, his hair changed from black to white, his skin lost some of its color, and his dark eyes became violet. "You do, it's just not my favorite form to take." He snapped his fingers again, his original features returning. "You can change your form at will as well." He flicked out a hand, gesturing at my face. "And you can stop with that whole monster nonsense. You're not a monster, Sloane. Never have been."

"Says the man who made me this way. I kill people, Azrael. How am I *not* a monster?"

He chuckled, shaking his head. "Name one innocent person you killed. Name a single one, and I'll agree that you're a monster."

Grumbling because he was right, I crossed my arms.

"Exactly. How many people have you saved because you took out the trash, Sloane? Because you did what I could not? Thousands? Hundreds of thousands? Each life you took had exponential ramifications. Exponential lives saved. And you call yourself a monster? No, daughter, you are not. A warrior, yes. A monster? Never."

As nice as those words were to hear, it didn't stop the betrayal that coursed through my veins. "Is that why you made me like this? To kill bad guys? Is that why you left me alone, left me to wake up with nothing and no one and no memory? So I could what? Be a warrior?"

Azrael flinched as if I'd slapped him. *Good.* I hoped those words hurt just as much as being left alone for a year. Just like waking up to the knowledge that my parents were dead. Did he even realize just how much I'd wanted to die? Just how much I begged for it? Just how many times I tried to make it so?

"It wasn't supposed to be this way," he whispered, his voice a gravelly mess. His gaze was beseeching, but it didn't faze me. One sorry expression wasn't going to erase the damage that had been done.

It wasn't going to take away what I'd lost.

"After I brought you back, I couldn't care for you like I wanted to. I was too run down, too weak. I needed to gather my strength. Celeste was supposed to look after you until I could, but she..." He trailed off, dipping his head to stare at his feet. "She couldn't. Aurora's death changed her. She isn't the same woman she was when she made her vow to me. But I didn't know that until it was too late. By the time I could come to you again, you seemed to be settling in."

*Settling in.* As if being homeless and alone was a good thing.

"I made sure Gerry kept an eye on you—not that he

could do much. When I was able, I did, too. You were finding your way, and it seemed wrong to interfere. And I didn't, until your brother posted that bounty on your head. Then, I had Gerry call his friends at the Night Watch. I knew Emrys Zane would never hand you over like chattel. Knew she would give you a job and a home."

A job and a home were only good if I didn't bring death to their doorstep. They were only good if I could keep them safe. And I didn't know how I'd be able to do that. If X had taken everything once, there wasn't anything to stop him from doing it again. An image played out in my brain. Instead of my father in a pool of blood, it was Dahlia and Simon. Instead of my mother giving me chest compressions, it was me trying to breathe life back into Bastian.

I shook my head, trying to get the scene out of my mind but it stayed there, imprinting itself like a brand.

"Why didn't you just let me die?" I choked out, as I tried to swallow a sob. I was going to lose them. I was going to lose them all.

Azrael gave a slight shake to his head, his gaze getting a far-off quality to it, as if he was staring at something I couldn't see. "You were meant for more—so much more than what you got. Your journey wasn't over yet."

My hands balled into fists at the utter nonsense falling from his lips. "What kind of vague bullshit is that? *My journey wasn't over.* According to who? Who gave you the right to change me? Who gave you the right to make me like this?"

*What good was my journey if I always lost the ones I loved?*

He snapped his fingers and a pair of black wings unfurled from his back, a wicked scythe in his hand as his eyes blazed purple. He kept the dark hair, though, which I thought was a nice touch. Still, if his end goal was to scare me, it wasn't going to work. My own brain conjured far more frightening things than a pair of wings.

Plus, what was he going to do, kill me? *Too late, Pops, I'm already dead.*

"*I* did," he insisted, flashing a double set of fangs that looked remarkably like the ones I saw in the mirror every day. "I gave myself the right. Because I see things that you can't or won't see. Because I've been around the block once or twice and know a couple of things you don't. Because you needed to be here."

In the next instant he shrugged his shoulders, and the wings went *poof* as if they'd never been there at all. "I swear, you and your sister are a handful. *No, Dad, don't keep me alive. No, Dad, don't tempt Fate. Please, Dad, save my ass from poltergeists.* Fates, it's as if you both are trying to die at this point."

A tiny buzzing took over my brain for a second before the base functions went back online. "I'm sorry, what? *Sister?* How many siblings do I have? I already know about the spawn of Satan. What is she, his evil twin sidekick?"

Azrael narrowed his eyes at me, likely unamused at the "spawn of Satan" remark. "Living? I believe just the two."

"*You believe?* Again, I ask, how many of us were there?"

"A lot. I'm older than time, Sloane. I've had a lot of kids. Though, I've lost many of them to war they waged with each other over a throne that was never theirs to take."

That shocked me enough to take a step back—which had me running right into Bastian's frozen form. "Please don't tell me I'm supposed to take a throne. I don't want a throne." I started shaking my head. "Nuh-uh, nope, no, not ever gonna happen."

"Don't worry, child. I have no plans to make you do something against your will."

That stopped me, and I met his gaze, narrowing my eyes. "That's not a 'no,' you know. I'm not dumb, Azrael."

He huffed out a chuckle that reminded me a bit of my dad's. "Oh, I know you're not." He sighed, pinching his brow as if I was giving him a headache. "Let me put it to you like this. I have no plans to give up my throne, but in the event I did, would you rather take it, or have the man who murdered your parents do it?"

"That's like asking me if I wanted constipation or diarrhea—either way my problem is still shit."

Azrael burst out laughing, tears of mirth on his face at my crude analogy. "You are so much like your sister, Sloane. I love that about you two. What strong women you've become after the challenges you've faced."

"She's like me?" Was that my voice? All small and childlike?

He nodded, a warm smile gracing his face, as if he was recalling a fond memory. "Same bravery, a few more scruples. She's a homicide detective in a town outside of Knoxville. A good woman."

A murderer has a homicide detective for a sister. That sounded like a disaster waiting to happen.

"But her power is nothing like yours, mostly because she's still alive. She is formidable, but you... You have yet to tap into what you can do. Your potential is almost limitless. I can teach you. I can help you."

While power seemed like a great thing, leaving the first place I'd called a home in far too long was akin to

X's knife in my heart. Reaching behind me, I clutched at Bastian's frozen hand. The flesh was still warm, still a reminder of what I had here.

"You must make a decision. Stay here or come with me to learn all you need to know."

Once again, both my options were shit.

## 19

"I'll give you time to think about it, but don't tarry too long. My son seems hell-bent on destroying you and your sister—just like he has done to the rest of my children. If I am to teach you all you must know, we don't have time to waste."

*Oh, now he's in a rush? Now he wants to twist the knife?*

Where the fuck had he been for the last year while I was sucking Rogues dry and digging graves? Where was he when I had no one and nothing but time? And did I still need to drink blood? Did I need to consume souls? How did I stop my face from flickering like a burning-out lightbulb?

There were too many questions and no real answers.

*How do I kill X? How do I find him?*

"I'll be in touch."

Rather than give me the answers I needed, Azrael gave me a smile instead, snapping his fingers and disappearing in the blink of an eye.

"Goddammit, Azrael," I yelled at the night sky. "You two-faced prick. You could have at least told me how to fix my face, you bastard."

Bastian's hand shook in mine, his body thawing upon Azrael's departure. Once again, I found myself behind his back, and a ball of fire graced his fingertips.

"Where is he?" Bastian hissed, his grip just a touch too tight. He was trembling, his fear not quite under wraps.

I put a quelling hand on his back, wrapping an arm around his middle as I rested my forehead between his shoulder blades. "He's gone. You can stand down."

Shaky breaths sawed in and out of his lungs, the adrenaline of it all causing him to crash a little. "He was so fast. I didn't think he would be that fast. But then again, he's Death."

"Quicker than a blink and just as ruthless as you'd expect," I murmured, reeling at how much and how little I'd learned from the encounter.

Bastian turned, cupping my cheeks in his hands. "Did you get any answers?"

My laugh was bitter as I shook my head, gently pulling my chin from his hold. "No," I replied, turning away from him. "All I got were more questions."

*And a choice to make. Don't forget you got that, too.*

But what kind of choice was it? I could leave the first home I'd had since my parents died to learn from a man I couldn't stand? Leave my friends, my... *Bastian* to play reindeer games with dear old dad? That sounded like a horrible plan, and a good way to start an apocalypse if I was being honest.

But how could I stay here when X was lurking around the next corner? It wasn't as if he didn't know where I parked my head at night. It wasn't as if he didn't know where I was. It wasn't as if he couldn't take *more* from me. Actually, he *could*. My friends were ripe for the picking if he got a bug up his ass to hurt me even more. How easily had he stolen Simon?

How easily had he infiltrated our home?

I stalked back to the house, the idea of leaving them burning in my gut. Leaving Bastian. A couple of months ago, I'd been all but begging to leave, and now, when I was presented with the choice, the mere thought of it felt like X's sword stabbing me on repeat.

"Sloane?" Bastian called, slowing my steps. "Do you want to talk about it?"

Did I? No, I absolutely did not. What I wanted to do was take him to bed and stay there. What I wanted to do was to kiss every inch of him and pretend the world didn't exist.

I pivoted on my heel, rushing him, though I hadn't meant to. His stunned arms caught me as I jumped, planting a kiss on his lips, which he quickly returned, only breaking it for a moment to answer him. "No, I don't want to talk about it. Can I request a make-out session followed by heavy petting and booze, though?"

"While I'm sure that isn't the healthiest way to deal with your problems, I'm not exactly going to say no." He hitched me higher on his hips. "I do want to talk about it at some point. The time where you had to deal with everything on your own is over. And not just me. Every single person in that house will be here for you—whether you ask for it or not." He swallowed, his Adam's apple bobbing. "I'm not the only one who loves you, Sloane."

My legs tightened around his hips, the urge to kiss him warring in my gut, along with the need to confirm what he'd just said. The uncertainty won out. "You... love me?"

I knew he wanted me, but I sort of figured what I felt for him was too much. Too soon. Too... just *too*.

"I'm pretty sure I've loved you since you bounced my head off the floor like a volleyball."

Chuckling, I shook my head. "Oh, so that's the brain damage talking, then."

Somehow, his hand found its way in my hair, fisting the strands in his fingers, bringing my mouth to his. My eyes fell closed in anticipation, but he didn't kiss me.

"Look at me," he whispered against my lips, and I forced my eyes open. "My mind is perfectly clear. It's not brain damage or me craving your bite, or any other excuse you can come up with to justify why I feel the way I do. I love your grit, your strength. I love your sense of honor, of justice." He sank his teeth in my bottom lip, soothing the bite almost as soon as he gave it. "I love you, and that's not going to change, no matter how many trials we face. Want to know why?"

I had to break his stare, those bottle-green eyes burning all the way down to my very soul. How could I accept such a beautiful gift when just me being here put him in danger?

"Yeah," I croaked, not wanting to hear the rest but needing it all the same. Tears flooded my vision as I brought my gaze back to his.

"Because I'm yours and you're mine, and that'll be true in this life or the next. Until the sun stops burning, understand? I'll repeat this as many times as I have to until you believe it."

The tears crested and fell, streaking down my cheeks, as the sweetest pain hit my chest. "I believe you."

And god help me, I did. Bastian wouldn't let me go without a fight, and there was no way I could stay here if I wanted him safe. But he had to know. I couldn't do what I needed to if he didn't. "You know I love you, too, right?"

Bastian gave me an indulgent smile, as if I was the one just now catching up. "I caught that."

For some reason that had me breathing a sigh of relief. "Good."

"Let's get you that order of heavy petting and alcohol, shall we? Then maybe we can come up with a solution. Yes?"

But I already had a solution—it was just going to kill me to do it. "Sounds good."

At that, he led me through the kitchen, stealing a bottle of vodka from the freezer and a couple of glasses before guiding me to his room. Along the way, I tried to memorize every bit of the house, every nuance of his movements, all the expressions on his face. When we made it to his domain, I didn't bother with the alcohol. I kissed him with every single bit of the love I had in that shriveled organ I called a heart.

His answering kisses were just as intense, just as powerful as mine. They scrambled my thoughts, made me believe that I could stay. Made me contemplate a future where we could be together. Where he would be safe from the danger that clung to me like a death shroud.

In my fevered imaginings, I saw a time where we were safe. Where we were happy.

But then the images of his lifeless stare as I tried to restart his heart flashed in my mind. He and I were never going to get a happy ending, and that only made me kiss him harder. Because if this was the last time I would have with him, I was going to show Bastian just how much I loved him.

My fingers found the hem of his shirt, deftly pulling it up and over his head. I needed his skin. I wanted to touch every inch of him, kiss everything I could reach. I wanted him to feel every ounce of pleasure he'd ever given me—give him *more*, and then some. I wanted his moans, his groans. I wanted his hisses and dirty talk.

I wanted everything.

Before long, we had stripped off all clothing, our frenzy making the night pass far too fast. We tasted each other, loved each other, and when we couldn't hold our eyes open any longer, we slept.

Just like the previous night, I woke before Bastian, but this time I didn't linger. I couldn't allow myself to get caught this time. Moving as silently as I could, I dressed enough to be decent and made my escape, heading straight for my room. The house was silent enough, and I was grateful for the plush carpeting that allowed my stealthy race through the hall.

Once I reached my room, I stopped my sneaking, racing for the closet. Quickly, I located the weekender bag full of old photo albums and Julie's ring. Slipping the cool metal on my finger, I felt a sense of dread wash over me.

He wouldn't know why I left him. Bastian would be in the dark. Was that better or worse than learning the truth? That I was exactly what Thomas had called me those few months ago.

An albatross.

A curse.

And I wasn't going to let him get dragged down with me.

The best I could do was rip a few clothes off the hangers, rummage in the drawers for underwear and socks, and toss the lot into the bag. Then, I dressed in what I figured was a durable outfit. Black jeans and a leather jacket, T-shirt and boots. Who knew where I was going, or how long it would be before I could get fresh clothes? After tying the laces on my boots, I snatched the handle of the duffle with all my worldly possessions and made for the desk.

I had to tell Bastian that I loved him. Had to let him know not to look for me. That I was safe—even if that was possibly a lie.

Unfortunately, I didn't get a chance to do anything of the sort. Especially since the man in question was standing right outside my closet with an expression like thunder. His gaze dropped from my face to the bag in my hand, arms crossing over his bare chest as if he'd run out of his room to chase me down.

"Going on a trip?" he asked, the whispered words slicing through the silence.

I swallowed, regretting getting the bag and the clothes. I should have just gone. I should have run out naked—something, anything. Anything that made it so I didn't have to see his face lose all expression. Anything that made it so I wouldn't glimpse the utter agony right before it turned to stone.

"You could say that."

Bastian pressed his lips together as he slowly nodded. *Oh, man, he's going to lose it.*

"So, love and trust are mutually exclusive for you then? You love me but you don't trust me. Why else would you leave before dusk?"

Blinking back tears, I searched the ceiling for answers. There were none.

"I'm going to get you killed," I whispered, my eyes

still aloft, not looking at him. If I spared him so much as a glance, I would wimp out, and for his sake, I couldn't do that. "We've gotten lucky so far, but one of these days, we won't. One of these days he's going to come in here and slit your throat. I'm going to watch you die. I'm going to watch *them* die. Azrael can teach me. He can show me what I need to know. And everyone can live without me. Everyone can be safe."

"What were you going to do? Leave a note? Some pitiful Dear John letter, explaining that talking to me was just too hard or some other toss? Did you think I wouldn't understand?"

"No. I didn't," I said, sighing and giving up my inspection of the ceiling. "Because I figured you'd be arguing with me, just like you are right now. Tell me— how old was my mother?"

Bastian seemed confused at my switch in topic.

"Emrys said she was a venerated blood mage, so how old was she when X slit her throat? How much power did she have—did she waste—protecting me? Do you know?"

He shook his head, but the answer didn't really matter.

"She was old enough to know what she was doing, and X still killed her right in front of me. Every time I close my eyes, I picture you laying lifeless on the floor, and I'm trying to bring you back, but I can't." I inhaled a shuddering breath, tears falling in earnest now. "Simon and Dahlia are dead, I can't find anyone else, and... If I can stop that, I will. If I can keep you from leaving this earth, that's exactly what I'm going to do."

He took a giant step toward me, his warm hands on my arms, infusing me with his heat. "Sloane, you just got your memories back. You just learned who and what you are. You have to take the time to process that before you do something rash."

I tried to contemplate just what that would entail, and a hysterical sort of giggle bubbled up my throat. "Honestly, I don't think there is enough time in the world for that mess."

"I told you that I would stick by you until the end."

And I believed him.

"But what good is that promise if you're dead?"

## 20

No matter what retort he could come up with —no matter what reason—I still had to leave him. So that's exactly what I did. Skirting around Bastian, I marched right for my bedroom door, squeezing the leather handle of the duffle so I didn't start screaming. Because that's precisely what I wanted to do. I wanted to scream and cry and throw a genuinely juvenile hissy fit.

Instead, I swallowed down my urge to break, the bitter pill shattering my heart, and I hadn't even left yet.

I made it to the landing before Bastian's hand was on mine, pulling me to a stop. "Please, Sloane. Just give me some time. Maybe—"

"There isn't time," I hissed. "He already knows where I sleep. And the attacks keep getting worse. If I don't go now, who knows what will happen? Maybe... maybe if I can get away, he'll leave you all alone." I shook my head, tearing my hand from his, the sheer agony of it burning me up inside. "I have to go."

I wanted to kiss him goodbye. I wanted to stall until the end of time, but I didn't.

*One foot in front of the other, Sloane. Keep moving.*

My mother's words were the last things I wanted in my brain, her memory stinging just a bit more now that I knew the truth, but her advice was still sound.

*Keep moving.*

And I did. One step after the other, one agonizing pain after the next. On and on until I was almost to the door.

"Where the fuck do you think you're going?" Thomas growled, barring my way, the midnight-blue door a beacon behind him.

"Yeah," Dahlia called from beside me. "I wanna know, too. It's like every couple months, your ass is trying to ditch us. What? We smell or something?"

Axel stepped up behind her. "Right? I swear, girlie, it's a pain in the ass, and I'm not rightly fond of pains in the asses."

Clem and Simon closed in with Harper trailing behind them, giving Thomas backup at the door. "Fun fact," Harper muttered, "most of the time, your emotions break even Emrys' warding. So, if you thought that living with you was sunshine and roses, you'd be mistaken. But I'd rather have you here on our side and deal with the utter hell going on inside your head than have you out there in danger. And just so you know, I only give a shit about a limited number of people in this world. You're one of them, so how about you stop trying to be the martyr, huh?"

My face was leaking, and I tried to wipe away the mess, but it was a losing game.

"What if you all get hurt because of me? I can't—"

"Oh, fuck what you can't," Harper countered, cutting me off. "You're not special. You think we haven't done this a handful of times with Simon? With Thomas? You think Axel's past is giggles and rainbows? Spoiler alert: none of us made Santa's nice list. We all have a past. We all have demons. One of these days, it'll be my turn to worry about my chickens coming home to roost. Would you let me leave? Would you let me go off half-cocked like a fucking moron?"

She didn't even give me time to say anything because she already knew the answer.

"No, you wouldn't. You'd hogtie me or knock me out or something because I was being a stupid bitch. Am I wrong?"

She wasn't, but I didn't want to tell her that. A faint

meow brought my gaze to my feet as Isis wound her skeleton self around my ankles, joining the party. Her glowing green eyes bore into me as if to echo Harper's sentiment. Groaning, I dropped my duffle and picked up the bone kitty.

"Fine, but—"

My words died on my tongue as Isis twisted in my hold, a familiar green mist wafting from her open mouth and into my nose. A couple of months ago, she'd done the same thing, only then, we'd been searching for Simon. A familiar premonition slammed into me: one I'd seen in Aunt Julie's memories.

*Night had fallen on a giant home set away from the city, clad with a gray stone façade, with elegant architecture and a midnight-blue door. Men surrounded the house, guns in their hands and spells on their belt, their tactical gear loaded down with magical weapons and enough potions to stop a rhinoceros—or an ancient vampire.*

*They blasted their way through a ward, their numbers too great for the magic to hold, spells firing right along with the guns. They had a singular focus, and it was not one of capture.*

*This was a kill order.*

*This was the end of the Night Watch.*

I was too late. I'd let them keep me here too long, and now there wasn't time.

"Get away from the door," I croaked, clutching the

cat to me as I tried to find my bearings. Part of Julie-slash-Isis' vision still blinded me as to what was around me. "Men are coming to kill us. Right now. I stayed too long. Oh, god, I stayed too long."

Arms surrounded me, guiding me to a chair. *Bastian*. His warm touch lent me comfort, love, even though I probably didn't deserve it.

"Tell me what you saw. Exactly," Thomas ordered. "Was it like last time?"

"And after you do that," Simon piped up, "tell me why my cat is giving you messages like that. Isis is my psychopomp, not yours."

I ignored Simon's plaintive grumbling to answer Thomas. "Yes, but I've seen this before. Julie saw this the day she died. Men are coming. Tactical gear and spells on their belts. Big ones—ones big enough to bust the wards."

"Harper?" Thomas called.

"Already on it. Engaging Ivory Tower protocol." Harper's voice took on a no-nonsense quality to it, as if she'd been preparing for this shit since the day she was born. "Clem, get Emrys, will ya?"

"Sure thing, Sugar."

Blinking furiously, the world slowly came back into focus, the images of the coming attack flashing like an echo over everything. I cuddled the kitty closer, waiting for my sight to fully return.

"Did you see how many? Where they're coming from?" Bastian asked, rubbing his hands over my chilled arms. Yeah, I was wearing a jacket in the middle of Tennessee spring, but I was freezing.

"Twenty or more. All magic-users. Full tactical gear. *Guns.*" A sob crawled up my throat. "I told Emrys this would happen if I stayed here. I warned her."

Part of me wondered if I called Azrael if he would help. The other part reminded me that he didn't seem too concerned about my welfare—especially since someone couldn't kill an already-dead woman.

"Yes, yes," the woman in question replied as she exited the dungeon door with Clem trailing just behind her. "And I told you then just like I'll tell you now, we'll figure it out." She turned to Dahlia and Simon. "Reinforce the Tower protocol. No loopholes or gaps."

Thomas stood from his crouch. "If these guys are anything like the ones who attacked the Dubois nest, they're going to have ward-piercing arrows. We need to be prepared for a breech. Anything that can cause true death needs to be armored up to the gills."

"Head to the armory then. Use the vests with the titanium plates and protective sigils, gorgets, the works.

Clem, get anyone anything they need. You have my permission to pull out the big guns."

Clem nodded her red head, her expression practically carved out of marble.

"Axel, follow her. Any weapon you can carry, yeah?" He nodded and took off, following Emrys' command. "You three, follow me. We'll need potions."

She led us to a bookcase—the entire downstairs was filled with them, hidden in nooks and crannies, anywhere and everywhere. It was like living in a library. Similar to the one in her office, she pulled a book's spine, and an audible click sounded. The case swung into the room to reveal a cache of weapons, potions, and you guessed it: more books. The bottles were varying shades of the rainbow, each with an odd glow that spoke of magic.

Emrys grabbed several at once and dropped them into a black canvas bag with a strange Celtic symbol on it. It was close to a traditional tri-knot only modified slightly, and I had no idea what it meant. She slipped the strap of the bag over her head before grabbing several that had leather thongs attached.

She handed Bastian and Thomas five each. "Stunning, paralysis, and torture potions. Don't miss." To me, she gave the rest. "Tie them to your belt. When you need it, snap the thong, twirl it three times, and launch. The first thing the potion hits is affected, so again, don't miss."

"Here," Axel called, his arms loaded down with weapons. Around his neck was what appeared to be a titanium gorget, the metal reaching just under his jaw and down to his collarbone. It made sense. Being a ghoul, Axel could only die if someone took his head.

I hoped Thomas would be donning something similar with a breastplate for good measure.

Someone passed me the whip Dahlia made just for me, and I strapped it to my thigh. Then it was a flurry of donning weapons and tying potions to my belt. I was more prepared for a battle than I'd ever been, and yet, I didn't feel prepared at all.

Because I'd seen this already. According to Julie and Isis, they were going to breech the wards—they were going to kill us. They were going to take everything away from me.

"Bastian," Harper called from the landing. "Get up here."

Without a word, he grabbed my hand, latching onto it before dragging me behind him. I'd never felt so frightened and so safe at the same time. Or so glad that his brain was following right along with mine. If we had to be in this fight, if we couldn't escape it, I wanted him right next to me at all times.

Just the thought of being separated practically gave me hives.

The pair of us hoofed it up the stairs, and Bastian unerringly led us to Harper's domain. I'd never actually been inside Harper's rooms before then, so I goggled at the wall of screens that displayed every inch of the Night Watch's compound save for the bedrooms and bathrooms. There were no windows in the space, just wall-to-wall screens, a desk filled with tall tumblers and bendy straws, and a cot with a small blanket and a lone pitiful pillow.

Compared to my room, this was practically "a cupboard under the stairs" situation.

"Quit it," Harper barked, yanking my gaze to hers. "I have a huge room next door, but this is where I work. And that's not why I called you up here. Look." She pointed to one of the middle screens.

On it was a handful of men in dark tactical gear— vests, helmets, body armor, the whole nine yards. Potion bottles swung from their belts as they advanced toward the front door. But instead of focusing on the giant guns in their hands or the caustic liquid in those vials, I lasered in on a vaguely familiar face.

"You know him?" Harper asked, and I nodded.

"I don't know from where, but he looks familiar." I glanced up at Bastian, ready to ask him if he recognized the man, but I stopped myself. Bastian's expression was pure, unadulterated rage, and his jaw seemed to be about a millimeter away from snapping in two.

"Jarek," he growled, his bottle-green gaze glowing brighter and brighter as the seconds ticked past.

That name sounded familiar, too, and I sifted through the last few days of shenanigans to place it. "The manager of the club? The one you fired?"

The one who tried to zap me to death for biting Bastian's neck? Yeah, I sounded incredulous, but come the fuck on. This guy didn't have the stones to fight his way out of a wet paper bag, let alone attack the whole of us together.

*Man, I should have killed that guy when I had the chance.*

## 21

"What I want to know is how he found us in the first fucking place," Bastian growled. "I thought this house wasn't even on a map."

Harper narrowed her eyes at the screen. "It isn't, and Emrys made it so even satellites can't see the house or the property, and I seriously doubt anyone broke her wards unless…" She trailed off, lost in thought. She shook her head, blinking rapidly. "Please tell me someone was smart enough to sweep Celeste before ya'll brought her here?"

Harper wasn't asking me since I'd been a crispy critter when I got back, but Bastian stared at her blankly as if his entire brain had been switched off. A sinking feeling settled in my gut. I hadn't taken a shine to

Celeste—mostly because she'd left me to fend for myself rather than offer me a single iota of help—but I'd sort of figured she was on my side. Her daughter had been taken away from her just like my family had from me.

But what if she didn't blame X like I did?

What if she blamed Azrael?

*Oh, shit.*

Bastian took off, racing out of the room and down the stairs, with me hot on his heels. But while he stopped at Emrys, I continued on to the dungeon. Shouts sounded behind me, but I kept moving. If Celeste was the catalyst, I needed to snuff her ass out post-haste.

How stupid were we? How easily had I been fooled by a sob story and a tearful tribute to a dead daughter? But had I? In the short time I'd been in her presence, Celeste had rubbed me the wrong way.

What if it had all been bullshit? What if my gut had been right about her?

The runes embedded in the bars and walls burned my flesh as the magic rose high on the air, just before the concussion of a cell door blowing off its hinges nearly knocked me off my feet. As the dust cleared, Celeste sauntered from her cell, a tranquil quality to her face as a swath of black magic billowed over her fingertips. She placed an open palm right on one of the still-burning runes, her flesh sizzling as she smiled. The runes flickered, her hand glowing like they once had.

I didn't understand until the runes dimmed, and her hand grew brighter. She was stealing the magic from the walls. *That can't be good, right?*

A thousand questions flitted through my mind, but the most prominent of them fell from my lips. "Why?"

Silly me, I'd have thought a woman who supposedly devoted her life to keeping X away would give a shit if I lived or died. Or maybe that was precisely it.

I was dead, but I was here.

And her daughter wasn't.

"Why wouldn't I?" Celeste asked, her calm smile such an odd dichotomy from the teary act she'd put on earlier. "I pleaded with Azrael to bring Aurora back when she died, but he refused. I begged him to kill me after you fell, but he wouldn't. But he brought you back, didn't he? He just snapped his fingers and gave you a piece of himself like it was nothing. Got you all cleaned up and handed you back to me with a pat on my head and a 'don't fuck it up this time' pep talk."

I couldn't help it; I pressed my eyes closed at the sheer stupidity of it all. It was as if Azrael had no idea what grief could do to a person, as if he had no clue what a woman with nothing to lose could do.

*Moron.*

I wanted to haul his ass down here and give him a piece of my mind. "I'm so sorry, Celeste. I wish…" I didn't know what I wished, but her situation was total bullshit. "I don't know how to fix this for you."

But I also didn't know what I was supposed to do. This house was about to be attacked—my friends killed —and she'd been the one that brought them here. Our own personal Trojan horse. And if I were to venture a guess, she was the most formidable of the lot. Giving her an ounce of leeway was going to tip the scales in her favor.

"Oh, but I do. I know exactly how you can fix this for me." The last of the runes winked out, the heat on the air dying like a doused fire. The house itself seemed to tremble in response, the pungent scent of burning metal and flesh permeating the small space.

"You can give that little nugget of Azrael's magic to me, or I can rip it from you. Really, it's up to you. How did you phrase it? Oh, that's right: 'I really don't give a fuck which.'"

A strange crackling sensation raced across my skin as I felt a spell behind me let loose. Smartly, I ducked, allowing whoever was at my back to have an open shot at the crazy witch. The magic hit Celeste but seemed to do nothing more than fizzle out before melting into her flesh.

In no way was that a good thing. In fact, I was pretty stumped on how I was supposed to kill someone that powerful without magic.

"Oh, how sweet. You've come to protect your stray," she taunted, a feigned pout on her face.

Emrys got between Celeste and me, her hand fishing in her satchel as magic bloomed over her fingers. "And you've signed your own death warrant." To me, she muttered, "Get back upstairs. I'll hold her off."

*Yeah, no.* There was no way I was leaving Emrys to deal with this bitch by herself. Celeste wanted something from me, and I had no doubt in my mind that she'd go through Emrys to get it if she had to.

"Tell me," I called, ignoring Emrys completely and positioning myself in front of her. "Does my father know what you're up to?"

Celeste snorted, rolling her eyes. "I doubt it. Azrael has always had trouble getting into my mind." She tapped her temple, taking a step forward. "You know that's how he picks his lovers, right? When he finds a woman he can't read, he goes gaga over her. Wining and dining. Gifts. The works. I really can't blame the man. I mean, if I heard a world's worth of thoughts, I'd shoot myself in the face. So, it's not a surprise that every time he finds a woman who can't mentally tell him just how mediocre he is by accident, he's all over that. Problem is, he keeps knocking them up and then ditching them for the next bitch he can't read." She tsked, shaking her head. "Rude."

*Ouch.* My father sounded like a fuck boy.

"So that's a no, then. Cool. Umm." At a loss for words, I called to Azrael in my mind. If he were so in tune with his children as she claimed, maybe he'd hear me.

*Did you hear that, Azrael? Your ex-side-bitch is the bad guy. Wanna help my friends and me not die?*

I didn't have high hopes that he'd come running.

"Of course, if you just give me what I want, I'd call the whole thing off. Me and my friends would pack up and head home." Celeste took another step toward us, swirls of black flitting over her fingers like live snakes. "And if you don't, I'll make sure every single one of you die screaming just like Booth did." She hummed happily, as if she relished the memory of Booth's torturous death. "He really took a long time to die."

Emrys latched onto my arm. "It's time to go, Sloane."

I agreed with my boss, but it was a question of getting out of here alive. I had a feeling anything we threw at her would just slide right off or get absorbed, or whatever the hell she was doing. If we ran, she'd just zap us, and I had no desire to die screaming. It was one thing to yell at Azrael about keeping me alive, but it was quite another to just hand myself over to a woman working with the man who killed my parents.

I barely nodded my head as I took a step backward. I needed a distraction that could get us the hell out of this dungeon. And again, how stupid was I?

*Yeah, Sloane, let's go into a room with only one exit with the bitch who brought these assholes to our door. Sounds like a real good idea. Stellar thinking.*

"Funny, I wouldn't think you'd work with the man who murdered your daughter. Tell me—what would Aurora think of you blithely partnering with her killer?"

The taunt had the exact effect, and Celeste wildly blasted off a spell in retaliation. In the commotion, I whispered the incantation to activate the whip, shooting it out as the ribbon of its power unfurled and slicing a cell door off its hinges.

*Magic won't work on her? Fine. Let's see how she handles a cell door to the face.*

Before she could release another shot, I had that door in my hands and launched it at her, watching with supreme satisfaction as she went down.

"Okay, now we can go," I announced, stowing the whip as Emrys stared at me as if I'd grown another head. "What? I wasn't going to leave you behind. Now let's bounce before—"

An enraged scream cut off my words, and I latched onto Emrys' hand, dragging her behind me as I raced for the dungeon's exit.

I was sort of hoping a cell door to the nugget would have at least bought us five minutes, but it didn't exactly surprise me that I wasn't so lucky. Or that Celeste had decided to toss that fucker right back at us. I had a feeling that damn door was going to hurt me a hell of a lot more than it had hurt her.

Before I could wrench Emrys up the last of the stairs, a hand clutched onto my forearm, yanking me up and through the door. Bottle-green eyes met mine before they drifted past me, giving Emrys a nod of his head.

A large push shoved my back at the same time, and Emrys slipped from my grip. I tried to tug my arm free from Bastian, but his hold was practically an iron manacle. Turning half my body back, I watched as the cell door froze midair, while Emrys gave me a sardonic raised eyebrow. With her newly freed hand, she twisted her wrist, and the dungeon door slammed closed, cutting her and Celeste off from the rest of us.

"Emrys," I screeched, trying to get back to the dungeon, but Bastian's iron grasp dragged me away and shoved me to the ground as a spell whizzed by my head.

It was then that I realized, that while Emrys and I were in the dungeon, a whole other battle had been going on in the living room. Taking shelter behind a tufted leather couch, Bastian and I stared at each other for one long second.

The sound of his voice echoed through my head, the shock of it hitting me with the force of a wrecking ball.

*Gods, I love this woman. How did I get so fucking lucky?*

It sounded so clear, it was as if he'd said it out loud. Honestly, if I hadn't been watching his face, I would have believed he had.

"I'm the lucky one," I said, pressing a hasty kiss to his surprised lips. "Now, let's stop these bastards before Celeste finds out how to break out of that dungeon."

The surprise morphed into understanding in a split second, and a small smile pulled at his mouth as Bastian gave me a nod. Multicolored magic swirled over his hands and up his arms as his smile grew practically malicious. Without another word, he stood, firing off a ball of electricity with one hand as a maelstrom whipped through the house with the other.

Yep, I was definitely the lucky one.

I just had to stay lucky.

## 22

D iving head-first into the fight, I unfurled the whip at my side, letting it loose on the first intruder with gusto. I was under no illusion that these assholes had come here for anything other than to kill us. For some reason, it didn't matter to me whether or not someone had tricked them into coming. These men were nothing like the ghouls who'd attacked us a couple of months ago.

These men weren't puppets. They hadn't been fooled into coming here.

So I felt exactly zero remorse as the whip sliced through a mage's arm like butter, the crackle of electricity on his no-longer-attached hand dying. He howled in agony for about three more seconds before I struck the whip out again, this time aiming for his neck.

My aim was true enough, and the poor bastard was dead before his head hit the polished wood floor.

The ground beneath our feet began to shake, and books rattled off their assigned shelves as the floor at our feet pitched and swayed. Wood snapped as the flooring buckled and jagged bits rose in the air, hovering for just a moment. And then I saw the mage holding them there, his nose bloody as if the strain was far too much for him. He met my gaze before offering me a sneering smile. He began to squeeze his hand closed but didn't quite manage it. All of a sudden, his eyes rolled up in his head, and his jaw twisted to the left, the sickening crack of his neck breaking reaching me all the way over here. The shards of flooring fell back to the ground like toothpicks.

I wanted to search for who'd saved my ass, but I ended up being too busy getting shot at and spelled that it took a minute. A bolt of electricity slammed me into a wall, white-hot agony racing over my flesh as another jolt hit. Growling through the pain, I attempted to peel myself from the shattered bookshelf jabbing me in the back as I scanned the room to locate where the stupid magic was coming from. Using the wood as a springboard, I sailed toward my assailant. In the commotion, I'd dropped my whip, but that didn't matter.

After all, I was feeling a bit peckish.

My fangs had a hell of a time sinking into his neck, though—what with all the body armor and all—so I settled on ripping his head off his shoulders instead. A knife flashed in my periphery, and I dropped the head in my hands, ducking at the same time. Said dagger caught the crest of my cheek, opening the skin there before I could retaliate. A wide-eyed sorcerer held the blade in a shaking hand as he eyed my face like he wished he could take it back. I suppose I should've felt a sliver of empathy for the guy, but I didn't. All I had coursing through my veins was wrath and a fair bit of malice.

Empathy wasn't on my radar, and it sure as shit wasn't on my to-do list.

My smile was wide as I gave the feeble intruder a push-kick to his knee, snapping it backward as he let out an unholy howl of pain. Catching his blade before it could hit the ground, I whirled, taking his head.

More and more mages trickled in, seeming to come from everywhere, and I took stock. Bastian was blasting a few mages off their feet in between swings of his sword—where he'd gotten it, I had no idea. Simon and Dahlia were on the stairs, holding steady on the first landing before the staircase, leading to the second floor. Black magic swarmed Simon as Isis yowled her displeasure from the upper landing. The man who'd just gotten his head lopped off started to rise, a shroud of dark magic seeming to pull him up by puppet strings. Before I could really comprehend what was going on, the dead man yanked a gun from his belt and began firing at his comrades, his aim top-notch for someone no longer breathing.

Dahlia was right beside Simon, tossing potion vials with one hand as she rotated the other in a magical flourish. Another intruder's neck snapped, and Simon continued his process of raising the freshly dead.

On the lower level, Clem was holding a shotgun, bracing it against her shoulder as she shot a guy in the knee. Not bothering with the body armor, she pumped the shotgun and fired another shot, this time hitting him right in the face. Bloody blowback sprayed her baby-pink 50s-style housedress, and at the sight of the blood, she began cursing a blue streak as she unnecessarily shot the dead guy again.

"You lousy, no-good motherfucker. This dress is vintage!" She shot him again for good measure before moving on to the next guy.

I couldn't see Axel, but I could hear him. Axel's Southern drawl echoed off of the hallways as he taunted an intruder with some insult about farmers and sheep. Thomas was missing as well, but the soundtrack of rapidly dying screams clued me in to his general vicinity.

Everything seemed well and truly handled until the dungeon door blew off its hinges, Celeste and Emrys sailing through it as they continued battling each other. Emrys appeared just as formidable as she always did while Celeste was bloody, her face a half-mask of burned flesh while one arm hung at her side listlessly.

That wasn't to say that she wasn't holding her own.

If anything, she was doing far too well for someone going against Emrys. Large furniture pieces shook before rising in the air and zooming toward Emrys like missiles. Before they could make contact, Emrys waved her hand and stomped a foot. The white glow of spent magic flashed across the hardwood as her foot made contact, the chairs and tables turning to ash. Emrys waved her hand again as if she was gathering the ash, and the burned shards of what used to be the living room furniture rallied together to bombard Celeste.

The ashes hit her like a fist, propelling her through the dining room wall.

But even as I took a deep breath, I knew it wasn't over. I was proved right not a moment later when the remainder of the dining room wall exploded, metal and wood flying into the living room like shrapnel. The explosion took everyone's focus for a split second, and that's when our upper hand turned.

Simon and Dahlia ducked, trying to avoid getting hit

by the blast. But as they took their eyes off their opponent, he sliced his hand through the air as if it was a blade. Ice flowed in my veins as I watched twin red smiles bloom on both of their necks, blood welling from their matching wounds.

Dahlia's eyes widened as she clutched at her throat, trying to hold in the blood. Tears welled and raced down her cheeks in those scant moments before her bronze skin paled, and her knees gave out as the life drained out of her.

Simon clutched at his own throat for a single moment before he reached for his friend, the magic in his fingers snaking through the air toward her. Neither his magic nor his hands reached their target. In the next instant, he, too, fell, following her down the stairs, the pair of them landing side by side, blood pooling in a matching halo around their heads.

An echo of a memory flashed over their still forms. The picture of my father and the image of my greatest fear seemed to merge, the truth of what I saw and what came to be hitting me all at once.

A scream erupted from my throat as I ran for them—to do exactly what, I didn't know—when something cut across my back. White-hot agony raced over my flesh, knocking me to my knees. But at that moment, I didn't care about who was trying to kill me.

All I cared about was my friends.

All I cared about was the slight possibility that I might be able to do something—anything—to fix it.

Another lash raked across my back, and I turned, ready to fight off whoever was keeping me from them. Instead, I ran right into a knife in my gut. I stared at the blade in shock before meeting the gaze of the man who put it there.

"Remember me?" Jarek's smile was wide as he twisted the blade and yanked it up. Pain like I'd never felt bloomed over me, stealing every thought, every breath. I knew without looking that the damage to my middle was enough to kill me if I weren't already dead.

My knees buckled, and the knife slid out as I fell from his grip. Jarek leaned down, putting his face right in front of mine. "You don't look so tough now, do you? Tell me—when you crushed my wrists, did you think I wasn't going to come for you? Did you think I'd just let you get away with it?"

I wanted to tell him to fuck off, but a cough stole my breath. Blood pooled in my mouth, practically drowning me.

"That's okay. You don't have to answer," he said, his snide voice making me want to tear into him, made me want to make it so he never talked again.

A loud boom sounded, and he looked away for a split

second. Taking the scant opportunity, I struck, my fangs ripping into his throat faster than he could fight me off. The flavor of Jarek's blood was akin to garbage and bad pennies, but it helped stave off unconsciousness. However, the images that accompanied his death would give me nightmares until the end of time. I would have to tell Bastian what kind of awful shit was going on in his back room.

But that was for later.

Shoving Jarek's rapidly desiccating body off me, I staggered toward Simon and Dahlia. Then a wrenching scream of the worst torment echoed through the room. Without turning, I knew the sound came from Bastian's throat, and the agony in it made me want to break.

But I did turn, searching for the man I loved in the middle of this war. Bastian's sword sliced through the mages like a hot knife through butter. He mowed them down in earnest as he made his way across the room. Explosions rocked the very foundations of the house, but none of that mattered to him. He was a one-man wrecking ball headed straight for his brother.

But his focus cost him.

It cost us both.

I saw the blade headed right for him before he did. It was small, almost dainty. The weapon sailed end over end as it rocketed toward the tender space between the armored plates at his side.

I never knew I could fear something so small. Never realized that such a tiny object could bring about my undoing.

The agony from my wounds left me as I raced for him, ready to take his place if I could. But the world seemed to slow, my feet molasses as they pounded closer but not close enough. The blade reached him before I did, hitting its intended target so much faster than I could.

Bastian met my gaze as he fell, those beautiful bottle-green eyes boring into me as blood bubbled from his mouth. Shock lit his face for a single second before sliding off, his expression falling away as the life slowly left him.

I reached him before he hit the ground, cradling him just like my mother embraced me right before X slit her throat—hugging him to me and praying as I put pressure on the wound.

All the noise faded away as I listened to his heart, the faint fluttering beats petering out as the breaths sawed from his lungs.

"No, please. Please. I'll give you anything. Please," I sobbed. "I love you. *Please.*" *Please don't leave me. Not when I've just found you.* My hands fluttered over his wound, over his chest. Nothing I was going to do would help him.

Bastian gasped, a deep pull of breath that sounded like pure torture, his lips mouthing, "I love you," before they stilled.

Then his chest followed suit.

And his heart stopped beating.

And then whatever soul I had left, left this earth with him.

## 23

There was a type of pain that couldn't be contained in a single body. No matter how powerful, no matter how old, losing a love like Bastian would destroy even the strongest of souls.

The scream that broke from my throat wasn't a sound that could be quantified or measured. It was torment and regret and misery. It was my soul shattering into a million pieces. Hot tears fled my eyes as I let my grief loose.

Maybe if I screamed loud enough, long enough, someone—anyone—would help me.

But there was no one to pray to and no bargain I could strike. If my father hadn't come by now, he wouldn't be answering my call. He wouldn't be coming for me or the man I loved.

I tried to clutch him closer, but Bastian's weight was ripped from my lap. My eyes popped wide, ready to battle anyone stupid enough to take him away from me, but no one was there.

And I didn't mean there wasn't someone who took his body. I meant no one as in, not a single soul was in the great room.

No Emrys or Thomas or Axel.

No Clem firing her shotgun.

No Bastian with blood on his lips, his beautiful eyes seeing nothing. No Simon or Dahlia, still as death.

The furniture that I knew for a fact had been blown to smithereens a few moments ago stood pristine in their rightful spots. The bookshelves were filled, each book untouched as if the battle had never taken place. But everything had taken on a shade of gray, as if someone had bled the color from the room while they were emptying it of people. The wall of windows at the back of the house showed a dark world where the moon didn't shine, and the stars had fled.

White motes fell from the ceiling, falling at an unhurried pace as if gravity had no hold on them.

*Is it snowing inside?*

I held out a hand to catch a snowflake just as I had as a child, the cold flake melting in my palm almost instantly.

This wasn't right. Where was everyone? If I was alive, shouldn't I be in the middle of a war right now? And if I was dead (like, *really* dead), where was Bastian? Where were Simon and Dahlia? If I was dead, shouldn't I be with him? And if I wasn't with them, where in the hell was I?

*You know where you are. You've been here before, haven't you?*

Images flashed in my brain of a grayed-out version of my living room, snow falling all around me as I sat on my couch. Azrael had come for me there, his crisp dark suit the same as when I'd seen him in the field. He held out a hand and told me to come with him—that he would make it better. That he would make it all go away.

*The In-Between.*

I was in the In-Between. Not heaven or hell—*if those places even existed*—but a place between worlds, between this life and the next one. Azrael had called it a holding area of sorts, a place where souls searched for the door to leave. This was where souls stayed until they moved on.

He'd told me so much while I'd held his hand, but most of it faded away as if the memory was playing keep-away with me. He'd been kind, so kind as he guided me to a blue door with an evil eye etched into the wood.

The memory faded as the living room flashed into color for a millisecond, sounds of the battle still going strong, a quick cacophony in the silence before snuffing out. The room went gray again, the silence a weighty buzzing around me.

I had to find Bastian and Simon and Dahlia. They were here. *They had to be.*

Because I wouldn't know what to do with myself if they weren't.

Pulling myself to my feet, I searched the great room like a woman playing a very macabre game of Hide-and-Seek. I looked behind furniture and hidden bookcases, but there was nothing but books and weapons to be had.

"Hello? Is anybody here?" I screamed, but no one answered me, the silence suffocating as it bore down on me.

Grief and panic warred in my gut, and I nearly sat down on the couch to breathe through the misery of it. Bastian was just here. Where was he? I had him in my arms.

*One foot in front of the other, Sloane. Keep moving.*

My mother's mantra stung more here than it ever had before. Because how was I supposed to put one foot in front of the other now? While I was in this gray place?

How was I supposed to breathe?

How was I supposed to find him?

*Keep moving.* My mother's voice grew insistent, as if she were whispering right in my ear. I spun, but no one was there. Then her voice called louder, more demanding. *Would he stop looking for you? Would he give a half-ass attempt at searching one room and give up? No. So why are you?*

She was right. Even if my own brain were supplying this pep-talk and not my mother, I couldn't give up now. I had the whole house, hell, the entire world to check. I had nothing but time, and I'd use every second to find him if that's what it took.

Racing to the dining room, I found a small woman with very familiar braids, sitting in her favorite spot at the opulent table. Her face was buried in her hands as she wept, grief spilling out of her.

"Dahlia?" I called. A small measure of relief threaded through me, blooming bright when her head whipped up at the sound of my voice.

"Sloane?" she said, scrambling from her seat to wrap me in a hug. "Gods, I couldn't find anyone. I thought... I don't know what I thought. How are you here? Are you dead, too?"

That was a question I didn't know the answer to—not really. "I don't know. Bas-Bastian—" I couldn't even say it, so I shook my head.

"Oh, no. Poor Simon. I can't imagine how much trouble he's going to get himself into to bring him back."

My heart broke all over again, and I had no idea how I would tell her that Simon was gone, too.

"Dahlia," I began, but she shook her head, stopping me.

"No, he's not." She backed up, running into the table before she stopped. "He's fine. Don't you tell me he's not."

The expression on her face mirrored mine, the ravaged grief of a woman losing her... Oh, no. I'd had no idea. Dahlia *loved* Simon—loved him more than anything. And that realization made what I had to do so much worse.

Swallowing hard, her grief made it so I could barely speak. "He died right beside you. You went together."

She knocked her braids off her shoulder, gritting her teeth against the pain as an expression that could only be described as livid settled on her face. "Well, then where the hell is he?"

I couldn't say why that one sentence made me laugh, but it did—the mirth buoying me out of the deepest grief waters. "I don't know, but I found you. Maybe we can find them. Maybe..." A plan started to form in my mind. "Maybe we can get out of here."

I was the daughter of Death, right? And I'd gotten myself here somehow, hadn't I? Then there had to be a way out.

Dahlia set her jaw and gave me a nod. "Let's go then."

For some reason, I grabbed her hand, not willing to let her go in this weird gray place. If she hadn't heard me screaming at the top of my lungs in the next room, I wasn't willing to chance letting her go.

We set off through the kitchen, searching for our men, the feeling that finding them would be the absolute least of our problems settling in my gut.

Unexpectedly, the kitchen was only mostly empty. A man stood at the sink, silently staring out the blackened window at the nothing beyond.

"Hey," I called, wanting him to turn while I had the pristine white island between us.

Startled, he glanced up, and it was someone I didn't recognize. *Or maybe I did.* Hadn't I taken his head? The man's eyes widened as he advanced, vaulting over the island like a pro. His hands reached for me as if he'd enjoy wrapping those fingers around my throat and squeezing whatever breath I had left out of me.

I let Dahlia go, and on instinct, I reached right back for the man. As soon as my fingers made contact with his skin, he began screaming as if he was burning. Light billowed out of his open mouth and eyes as his skin charred almost instantly. In less than a blink, the man had burned up in my hands like dry kindling, images of his stained soul hitting me all at once. Death. So much death at his hands. He'd lived too long, caring nothing of the people around him as he exacted petty acts of revenge and thoughtless transgressions.

Black grains of ash fluttered from my fingertips to the floor, and all I could think was, *good riddance.*

"Woman, what the fuck?" Dahlia barked. "You grabbed my hand like nothing when you knew you could do that?"

I shook my head. "I didn't know. I've never done that before. But it was similar to when I drank them down topside." *That was precisely it.* Only here, I didn't even need to read their blood to know and to reap horrible souls. "I don't think I can do that to good people. That's why I didn't hurt you."

Dahlia's skepticism was plain as day, but she put her hand in mine.

I repeated Azrael's words to her, hoping they gave her a small measure of comfort in this gray place. "I'm going to fix it."

I just hoped I was telling her the truth.

Abandoning the kitchen, we searched the mudroom and the garage but found no one. Exploring further, we hiked up the stairs, calling their names as we went. Maybe if they heard us, they'd come running.

The world flashed into color again as men I didn't know fought at the top landing, one smashing the other through the solid wood railing before they were gone again, the world losing its color.

Something told me we were running out of time.

"Why were you at the table?" I asked, trying to think of something—anything that would lead us to them. "Is that where you woke up or..."

"Yeah." Dahlia nodded, squeezing my hand at the memory. "I knew I was dying, felt myself go, and then I woke up in my favorite chair."

I had to wonder if where she woke up was special—if it meant something to her. And if that's where she woke up, then maybe Bastian or Simon might be where they were the happiest.

"Tell me—where is Simon's favorite place?"

Dahlia shook her head. "I don't know. I would say his room, but that was only because he couldn't go anywhere else for so long. Now that he's free, I don't know where that is anymore."

I shrugged, not able to think of a better place to look. "Can't hurt to check, right?"

I didn't know Bastian well enough to assume his favorite place, but I had a few ideas—that was if his preferred spot was in the house. If it happened to be outside, or anywhere else in the world for that matter, I was screwed. And a part of me didn't want to find him first.

If I found him before Simon, something told me it would be very, very bad.

## 24

"Let's just check everywhere, yeah?" I muttered, dragging her behind me as I headed for Simon's bedroom.

The door with its jaunty "No Girls Allowed" sign was ajar, and I braced myself for what I might find as I pushed it open. A distressed Simon paced back and forth in front of his beat-up leather couch. He had his beanie in one hand as he ran the other through his mop of black hair.

"Where is she? She should be here," he muttered, shaking his head, still not seeing us. "She was right beside me. She's supposed to be here."

"Simon?" Dahlia called, and the look on Simon's face when he glanced up was a thing of beauty.

He raced for her, and she let go of my hand, allowing

herself to be wrapped up in his arms as he peppered her face with kisses. "Oh, my beautiful flower. Where have you been?"

He didn't give her time to answer, her shock at his reaction plain as day. No, Simon just planted a kiss on her lips as if he'd been wanting to do that for ages, sifting his fingers into her braids as if he'd been dying to touch them and hadn't let himself.

I glanced away, the joy in them finding each other almost too much for my battered heart. I turned my back, giving them the privacy they needed.

"I thought I was in Hell," he whispered. "I thought I was back to being remanded to this house forever. Only this time, it was worse because you weren't here."

Was that how I'd view the world if I couldn't find Bastian? Probably.

"Okay, guys, I'm glad you found each other and all, but I need to find..." I couldn't say his name, not out loud, anyway. "I need to find him."

Simon's room flashed in color. Far-away sounds of fighting echoed through the room before silence and gray came back.

*No time. We had no time.*

"What the hell was that? Where are we?" Simon asked, clutching Dahlia to him as if he'd never let her go.

"The In-Between. Now hold my hand while I look for your brother."

Simon didn't say anything else, he simply grabbed onto my hand as I led us in an odd little march to Bastian's room. We had only spent a few nights—or days, rather—there together, but maybe he would be there. Maybe I'd get lucky.

I opened his door to reveal a messy bed. A messy, empty bed.

The bitter disappointment was hard to swallow, but I refused to stop searching. I let Simon's hand go as I raced for the bathroom, hoping for some nugget of good fortune to smile down on me.

Sitting in the empty tub fully clothed, Bastian slowly looked at me, confusion on his face. "Sloane?"

Relief flooded my limbs, and I dropped to my knees beside the tub. I reached for him, needing to make sure he was real and not just a fever dream. Our lips collided, and I nearly broke apart, I was so happy.

*I found him. I found him.*

Bastian broke our kiss. "Wait. Why are you here? I thought I was dead. I thought..."

"You are. I came for you. I don't know how I got here or how to get back, but I couldn't—" I shook my head, unable to describe the sheer agony of losing him. "I found Simon and Dahlia, too. I'm going to get us out of here. I don't know how yet, but I'm going to fix it, okay?"

Bastian brushed my hair off my face, cupping my cheeks. "I know you can, love."

The world flickered into color again, and Bastian's bottle-green eyes began to glow before fading once more. The color stayed longer each time, and I couldn't help but think that was a bad thing.

"We have to go." I got to my feet, and Bastian followed me, clasping my hand in his.

When we got back to the room, Simon and Dahlia were hugging each other, seeming lost.

"Guys?" I muttered, but they stared right through me until I put my hand on their entwined arms. Both of them blinked at me in surprise.

"Oh, thank fuck," Simon muttered. "You left, and we couldn't see you anymore."

The whole of the house seemed to pitch under our feet, and the world flashed into color, the sound seeming to turn all the way up. But it didn't flicker back. Something told me we weren't back. Something told me I needed to move, and now. "Yeah, we need to get the fuck out of here while we still can."

Gripping Bastian's hand, I pulled them from the room, racing back to where I came from. People milled about, no longer fighting but not seeing us, either.

Harper sat at the top of the landing, her head in her hands. She was sobbing, and the people around her had their heads bowed, giving her a wide berth. Everyone except Axel, who sat right next to her but not touching —like he wanted to but knew it would cause problems.

Our little group skirted around them, and Harper's head popped up, unerringly finding me.

"Please come back," she pleaded, staring right at me. How she saw me, I had no idea. I wasn't even sure she could see me. It was totally possible she could just feel me.

But with no time, I only nodded, dragging my friends down the stairs with me. At the bottom of the steps, Clem had Simon's head pillowed in her lap, black tears falling from her cheeks as she sifted a hand through his hair. With the other, she clutched Simon and Dahlia's joined hands.

On instinct, I grabbed Dahlia and Simon, guiding them back to their bodies. Fear clouded Dahlia's face, but I gave her an encouraging smile. "It's time to go back now."

Simon only held onto her hand, tugging her into position. "I'll see you on the other side, love. Don't worry."

Reluctantly, she laid down over her body, falling into it. The next second, the gash in her throat closed, and she sat up with a gasp. Simon quickly followed her, falling into his own body and rising a second later.

Clem startled before giving relieved hugs to them both, as Axel and Harper raced down the stairs.

"It's your turn," I murmured, pulling Bastian by the hand to his body. But unlike his brother, he wasn't so easily convinced.

"How are you getting back? What if—"

I raised up on my tiptoes and kissed him. "I think I'll be fine. It's time for you to go."

He dropped another kiss to my lips, reluctantly letting me go before doing as I asked. He went back to his body, falling into it just as everyone else had, but he didn't rise right away. My heart fell as a blistering doubt slammed into me.

*Please, please, please. Please don't let him leave. Please don't take him from me. I'll do anything. Please...*

Several long seconds passed, the wait to see his chest moving seeming to take eons. And then Bastian, too, gasped awake. His head whipped this way and that, searching for me as his gaze slid right through me.

"Where is she?" he shouted, but no one answered him.

Emrys knelt at his side. "Where is who?"

"Sloane. She was right there. She brought us back."

Emrys nodded, rising to her feet, drawing the sword

from the scabbard at her back. "She'll come when she finds the door."

Emrys moved to a tableau I'd failed to notice. Ingrid and Thomas held a squirming Celeste as the bound woman screeched and thrashed. Ingrid had a hold of Celeste's dark hair, keeping her head still so she could do nothing but stare at Emrys.

When the hell had Ingrid gotten here?

I glanced around, noticing the men and women that milled about weren't mages. They were vampires. Had Thomas called in a favor?

"Do ya have anything to say for yourself?" Emrys asked Celeste, her grip tightening on the hilt of the sword in her hand.

Celeste sneered before trying to spit at Emrys in lieu of answering. Unfortunately for her, Ingrid shook her by the hair, hard, making the spittle land on her chin instead.

"So be it, then." With a flick of her hand, Emrys took Celeste's head, the sword moving so fast I wouldn't have believed it had if Celeste's head weren't dangling from Ingrid's fingers.

Celeste's soul stood where her body had been before it fell to the side, confusion on her vile face as the world fell away, turning gray once more. Everyone around us had disappeared as we landed solidly in the In-Between.

Cracking my knuckles, I very nearly smiled, ready to reap this woman so there was no chance of anyone at any time bringing her back. But before I could reach her, Azrael appeared right in front of me.

His back to me and wings spread wide, the Angel of Death was out in full force.

"Azrael," Celeste exclaimed, reaching for him. "Help me. These awful people—"

He took a step back to avoid her hands, his wings retracting to reveal the smooth back of his suit jacket. "Save your pleading for someone who doesn't know the truth, Celeste. Tell me—how does it feel to betray your own daughter?"

"How does it feel to betray your son?" she shot back. "I'm not the only one you left behind, Az."

My father shook his head. "I didn't leave you behind, Celeste. We ended our relationship after you insisted on my son taking my job so I could play house with you. I told you from the beginning, I couldn't do that."

"Essex Drake is twice the man you are," she spat, taunting the man as if she wasn't boarding on a one-way trip to Hell.

Azrael chuckled mirthlessly. "Essex is a sociopath who murders innocents for fun. Just like he murdered our daughter. Just like he murdered her parents," he hissed, tossing a thumb at me. "He sent you on a fool's errand to kill a woman that cannot be killed. You chose the wrong side."

Without another word, he grabbed her by the upper arm. Almost instantly, Celeste's skin blackened like dying embers as light poured from her screaming mouth. I had to admit, her shrieks of pain were nearly as satisfying as if I'd have done it myself.

Azrael's wings reappeared, and he beat them once, a smile on his face as she broke apart. When she was nothing but embers floating in the air, he turned to me.

"You have stayed in my domain long enough. It's time for you to go," he said, gesturing to a door that seemed to appear out of nowhere, with an evil eye etched into it.

"But—"

He held up a hand, shushing me. "I know you have questions, and I'll answer them later. For now, you have to go."

For once in my life, I didn't argue. Why would I? Bastian was on the other side of that door.

As fast as I could, I reached for the knob.

"Sloane?" he called, and I turned back to him. "When you meet your sister, be sure to tell her X's name, will you? Tell her that I'm sorry I didn't give it to her sooner."

Understanding dawned. "You didn't want to kill him."

Azrael met my gaze, his filled with shame. "I should have, but I couldn't. So many people have lost their lives because I couldn't."

I nodded, trying to tamp down the rage boiling in my gut. Betrayal surged in my veins before reason took hold. Could I even fathom taking my child's life? Could I fathom letting that child take others from me? But those were answers I wouldn't be getting—at least not right now.

"Just for grins, what's my sister's name?"

Azrael swallowed, bowing his head in shame. "Darby. Her name is Darby Adler."

## 25

Walking through a mystical door from another realm to pop up in the middle of the living room kind of had a way of shocking some people. Which was how I ended up with Emrys' blade at my throat and almost attacked by a tiny blonde vampire. Ingrid realized who I was far faster than Emrys did, skidding to a stop right before she tackled me.

I met my boss' glowing red gaze with a look of irritation, plucking her blade from the side of my throat. "Is that how you say welcome back? Because we need to work on your hospitality skills a bit."

"Jesus, Mary, and Joseph, Sloane," she said before wrapping me up in a hug. "I thought I'd lost you."

I couldn't help hugging her back. It reminded me of

one of my mom's hugs, and I had to swallow down my tears.

"Thank you for bringing them back to me," she whispered. "I can't tell you how much I—" Her voice broke, and she squeezed me tighter.

"Yeah, well, don't get used to it. Me bringing them back was not a freebie invitation to do dumb shit. Finding their asses took work, patience, and a level of fuckery I was not exactly comfortable with."

My tirade had the intended effect of making her laugh, which allowed me to break the embrace. As good as it felt to be hugged, I wanted to find Bastian.

I'd barely gotten out of Emrys' arms before the big man barreled into me, sweeping me up in his embrace. Now that we were in the real world, his warmth seeped into me again, easing my soul. I eagerly clutched him to me, relishing the feel of his skin against mine. Just the breath in his lungs was a wish being granted.

"I was so worried," he whispered against my lips. "I thought you weren't coming back."

Just the thought of leaving made me want to cry, so I shook my head, kissing him with everything I had in me. There wasn't going to be a time where I would be able to leave Bastian. I knew that now.

"I'll always come back to you," I promised once our kiss ended. "Always. Do you understand?"

Bastian chuckled, holding me closer. "You went to Hell for me, Sloane. I think I believe you."

But I hadn't gone to Hell for him. I was pretty sure that little pocket world was a cakewalk compared to what was beyond. Granted, if Bastian had been sent to Hell, I would be on the first train downstairs.

"And don't you forget it."

"What?" a small voice griped. "No hug for me? I come in here and save the day, and not even a 'thank you'?"

I released Bastian to greet Ingrid, who didn't even have a speck of blood on what appeared to be a Catholic school uniform, her pale-blonde hair in plaits. "Hi, Ingrid. Thank you for saving our asses, though I'm pretty sure I missed that part."

Given the state of the living room, or rather the mounds of ashes piled up everywhere, our backup had been busy.

"It's okay. I'll lord it over you later."

I was sure that would be a super-fun time, too.

Several more people joined our little party, and pretty much everyone supplied hugs. Axel nearly broke my back as he squeezed the life out of me. "Remind me to get you any kind of blood you want. I swear, darling girl. I owe you big time."

"No problem, Axel," I croaked, patting his big shoulder. "It was no big deal."

Axel shook his head. "No, girlie. You did a good thing no one else could do, and all of us owe you until the end of time. Anything you need, anytime. Got it?"

"She gets it, Ax," Harper grumbled, shoving him out of the way. "My turn."

She advanced, ready to hug me, but I backed up a step, avoiding her touch. Harper told me once that touch made any warding completely worthless, and I didn't want to cause her harm.

"Don't worry about it," she said, the smile on her face wide and open, a first for Harper. "We're all happy here. It's okay."

Reluctant but unwilling to say no to her, I gave the small woman a hug, careful not to squeeze too tight.

*All my friends are safe. They are here and safe and happy, and I can hug them today.*

Harper's thoughts spilled into my brain, and I squeezed her tighter, the utter joy in those thoughts breaking my heart just a little.

She let me go first, tears gathering in her eyes, even as she gave me a wide grin. I wanted to say something, but I was attacked by the duo of Simon and Dahlia. The pair swarmed me in squeezes, and I couldn't help the relief at feeling them alive.

"I can't believe that shit worked. I swear, the 'go back into your body' trick only works in movies." Dahlia pulled back to stare at me, smooshing my face in her hands. "I can't say thank you enough."

"All right, all right," Bastian grumbled, peeling Dahlia's hands off my face. "Give Sloane back to me before you break her." He wrapped an arm over my shoulder, tucking me into his body.

Cuddling closer, I met Thomas' gaze through the throng. He gave me a regal nod, mouthing the words, "I owe you," before giving me a two-fingered salute. All I could muster was a tired smile and a shrug, the day's events catching up with me.

If Thomas felt he owed me, I'd let him. Maybe he could pay me back by helping me kill my no-good brother. That would be fun for everyone, right?

What was not a fun time was the clean-up process after the battle. Though Ingrid did know of an arcane company specializing in such things, letting them in the door was a problem. After the note drama on top of the whole siege shenanigans, no one was comfortable with anyone we didn't know coming into the house. Or being on the property. Or being within sniffing distance of the outer border.

So I was stuck helping out. *So much for everyone owing me big time.* Apparently, owing me did not encompass the utter ass pain of putting our house back together.

Fun fact: cleaning blood from hundred-year-old hardwood was a bitch and a half.

Granted, magic had handled most of the grunt work —restoring furniture and walls—but on top of consuming souls like it was my new day job, I was stuck scrubbing the landing like I was Lady fucking Macbeth.

I was about to give up on the whole deal and suggest replacing the flooring when the doorbell rang. The shock of it had me slipping in soapy water and landing on my ass. In the few short months I'd lived here, exactly zero people had ever come to the front door. Other than prisoners and a siege, there had been no visitors at all. I glanced up the stairs, and there was no Harper sticking her head out at the top of the landing to warn me, so I figured it might be fine?

Okay, I was wary as hell, but if anyone was going to answer the door, the person who was already dead was probably the best bet.

Reluctantly, I headed for the door just as the bell rang again, my pace less than urgent. Taking a deep breath, I twisted the knob and opened the door. On the stoop were three people—two ladies and a man. One of the women and the man I knew, but the other—a tall blonde—I did not.

"Agents Kenzari and La Roux, right?" I asked, instead of a more cordial greeting, my tone glacial. I hadn't just made it through an all-out siege followed by a trip to the In-Between to get hauled off to jail. I stepped from the house and closed the door behind me, crossing my arms as I faced them. "How can I help you?"

Agent Kenzari gave me a warm smile, likely intended to ease my nerves, but the effect was dashed by the stone-faced man at her back. Funny, he hadn't seemed so bad a couple of months ago, but now? Now he was a wall of no-nonsense with a "I'll eat you for breakfast" chaser.

"Sloane? Is your name Sloane?" the blonde woman asked, and I shifted my gaze from the agents to her. At my diverted attention, the man edged closer to her, as if he was ready and willing to spirit her off at the slightest provocation.

The woman I didn't know was tall and slender, with shocking cornflower-blue eyes and an open face. It was a face that made me want to tell her my secrets, and I didn't even know the woman.

*Get it together, Sloane.*

"Maybe. And you are?"

The woman smiled just a little before holding out her

hand to shake. When I didn't take it, she frowned a little before her smile came back in full force, a hopeful expression now stamped all over her.

"My name is Darby, and I think you're my sister."

My sister was a homicide detective *and* friends with ABI agents?

Yeah, there was absolutely no way that could go wrong.

*Sloane's story will continue with*
**Grave Watch**
*Soul Reader Book Three*

## DEAD CALM

*Grave Talker Book Three*

**There's not enough coffee or tacos in the world to deal with Darby Adler's family.**

If it's not her death-dealing father, her back-from-the-dead mother, or her ghost grandfather, it's her long-lost siblings and their bid for power.

With ABI radio silent and her siblings to find, Darby's got a major problem on her hands. Especially when the local coven figures out that her father's no longer bound.

**Can Haunted Peak, TN handle this family reunion?**

*-Preorder now on Amazon-*
*Coming June 29, 2021*

## GRAVE WATCH

*Soul Reader Book Three*

**Meeting long-lost siblings should be awesome, right?**

Well, when you happen to be on the wrong side of the law and have every intention of staying there, having a cop for a sister isn't exactly ideal. And teaming up with said sister? Well, that is just the cherry on top of the craptastic pie that has been my life.

But when our brother decides to attack us head on, banding together is the least of our problems.

**Because in our family? Being the hunter also means being the hunted.**

*-Preorder now on Amazon-*
*Coming September 28, 2021*

# THE PHOENIX RISING SERIES

*an adult paranormal romance series by Annie Anderson*

Heaven, Hell, and everything in between. Fall into the realm of Phoenixes and Wraiths who guard the gates of the beyond. That is, if they can survive that long…

*Living forever isn't all it's cracked up to be.*

**Check out the Phoenix Rising Series today!**

JOIN THE LEGION

EXCLUSIVE SNEAK PEEKS,
GIVEAWAYS, BOOK DISCUSSION.
COME FOR THE BOOKS.
STAY FOR THE MEMES.

To stay up to date on all things Annie Anderson, get exclusive access to ARCs and giveaways, and be a member of a fun, positive, drama-free space, join The Legion!

# ABOUT THE AUTHOR

 Annie Anderson is the author of the international bestselling Rogue Ethereal series. A United States Air Force veteran, Annie pens fast-paced Urban Fantasy novels filled with strong, snarky heroines and a boatload of magic. When she takes a break from writing, she can be found binge-watching The Magicians, flirting with her husband, wrangling children, or bribing her cantankerous dogs to go on a walk.

To find out more about Annie and her books, visit
www.annieande.com